RUFFIAN

RUFFIAN

Precious McKenzie

BeaLu Books

Author's Note

This is a work of historical fiction. Meg and her family are fictional characters. Frank Whitely, Jacinto Vasquez, Mike Bell, Barclay Tagg, John Sosby, Minnor Massey, Yates Kennedy, Vince Bracciale, Nick Lotz, Dan Williams, Squeaky Truesdale, and the Janneys were actual people involved in Ruffian's life. The representations of them are fictional yet are based on actual accounts gathered from interviews and racing archives. In all other respects, any resemblances to persons living or dead, events, or locales are entirely coincidental.

ISBN: 978-1-7353641-0-0 (Hardback Edition)
ISBN: 978-1-7353641-1-7 (Paperback Edition)

Library of Congress Control Number: 2020944525
Publisher's Cataloging-in-Publication Data is on file with the publisher.

Editor: Luana K. Mitten
Editorial Assistant: Madison Greve
Book Cover and Design: Tara Raymo • creativelytara.com
Cover painting of Ruffian: Henry Blond

Printed in the United States of America

BeaLu Books
Tampa, Florida

www.BeaLuBooks.com

Photo Credits: Cover & Page 201: ©nadiia; Page 191: © Adam Coglianese, Track Photographer, of the New York Racing Association; Page 196: © Associated Press; Page 198: © GeptaYs; Page 199: © Mick Atkins

for my mother and father

Table of Contents

Chapter 1: A New Life 1

Chapter 2: Out of Sorts. 16

Chapter 3: Meet the Family 20

Chapter 4: A Proposal. 26

Chapter 5: Hello, World!. 33

Chapter 6: Finding a Name. 38

Chapter 7: Goodbye, Mama 50

Chapter 8: Promotion 54

Chapter 9: Yearling Training 61

Chapter 10: The Training Track. 73

Chapter 11: South Carolina Bound. 79

Chapter 12: Attitude Adjustment 84

Chapter 13: Out of Control 93

Chapter 14: Job Interview. 95

Chapter 15: Horse People 101

Chapter 16: The Jockey 107

Chapter 17: Chica in Trouble 117

Chapter 18: On the Road 125

Chapter 19: The Maiden Race. 135

Chapter 20: The Fashion Stakes 143

Chapter 21: The Summer of 1974 148

Chapter 22: Off. 158

Chapter 23: Rest 161

Chapter 24: Back in Camden 168

Chapter 25: To the Races 171

Chapter 26: Match Race 174

Chapter 27: Emergency. 178

Chapter 28: And So It Goes 183

Chapter 29: Friends. 187

Epilogue 192

Bibliography 206

Note on the Author. 210

ACKNOWLEDGMENTS

For their kind, supportive, insightful feedback, I thank Edith Hemingway, Beth Ann Bauman, and Lesléa Newman. To my workshop friends, especially Amy Foos Kapoor, Stacie Ramey, Steven Dos Santos, thank you for cheering Ruffian to the finish line. My deepest gratitude extends to many people in the creation of this book. The research librarians, especially Roda M. Ferraro, at Keeneland Library provided most of the primary archival sources about Ruffian. Thanks to Amy who believes in field trips and the enthusiastic staff at Churchill Downs one early spring morning during Justify's morning workout before the Belmont. It was the chance of a lifetime to look a champion in the eyes. And, to my horse people, Jacqueline Dundas, Amy, Scott, Elise, and Evan Neuman, Penni Nance, Amy and Dana Cebull, Katie Holland, Linda Cebull, Amanda Kurdma-Potts, and many other good people who have doctored my own horse, gone on rides, or helped with Pony Club, thank you. To Jacinto Vasquez, Frank Whiteley, Mike Bell, Minnor Massey, the Janney family, Yates Kennedy, and to all of the people who looked after Ruffian. Thank you. I hope I served her memory well.

CHAPTER 1
A New Life

January 6, 1972
Lexington, Kentucky

"I will not wear that hideous dress!" Meg Murphy stomped her foot down and scowled at her mother. Meg's bedroom floor was riddled with discarded jeans and blouses. On her dresser rested a dusty cowboy hat.

Her mother, primly attired in a beige skirt and matching sweater set, complete with a complementary scarf, wrinkled her nose. "Meg, sweetie, it's your first day of high school. Wear something presentable."

"For Pete's sake, Mother, I'm not going to church. I'm going to school. Nothing wrong with jeans." She reached for the Wranglers on her bed. Mom intercepted her and folded them into her arms.

"Absolutely not. This is your first day. New school, new friends, new clothes. I won't have anyone in this town thinking we're a bunch of po-dunk ruffians from backwoods Montana." Mom paused, putting her balled up fists on her hips. "We need to get in with the right crowd here."

Meg snorted. "The right crowd? That's such B.S."

"Language!" Mom shrieked. *As if she'd never heard a curse word before. Please.*

Enjoying the squabble, Meg egged her on. "Oh, and by the way, we are po-dunk ruffians from backwoods Montana. Care to remember?"

Mom's face turned red with frustration. "Why do you always put up such a fight with me?"

Meg jutted her chin out.

"Fine. Be stubborn. You win, Miss Smarty Britches. Put on those dungarees. See how these society girls in Kentucky treat you." Mom turned to leave the room. She paused and smoothed her sweater over her skirt. "Meg, I just want to help you. I'm tired of fighting with you."

Meg bit back her anger. Why put on a show for these people? What did they care about her? She was who she was and she wasn't planning to temper it down for no one. Those folks could take her or leave her for all she cared.

"If you go waltzing into school in your old barn clothes, they're going to destroy you." With that, Mom walked away.

Meg tossed the polyester dress onto the canary and cream shag carpet. After bickering with her mother, Meg was in no state of mind to waltz into a brand new school. She was angry. Angry at trying to fit within this beige, blah world her parents took her to. A world of Bridge Clubs and tee times. Blah beige like her mother's matching twin sweater set. Beige that screamed blend, mix, don't stir or be noticed. Be a *good* girl. Don't fuss when things don't go your way. Beige, beige, beige. Meg longed for her home. Those wide-open bluebird days back in Montana where the colors of the sky sang out to her. Electric pinks refracting on the rimrocks at sunrise. Cloud shadows rolling over, darkening and cooling the prairie grasses in the heat of a summer afternoon. Atomic tangerine sunsets. She wouldn't cry. Not now, not right before school.

I need music, she whispered to herself, *mighty good music that will clear my head*. Flipping the switch on her record player, John Denver's warm voice soothed her as the 45 spun round and round. She softly sang along, "Take me home country roads, to a place where I belong," as she rifled through the tumble of clothes on her bedroom floor. She dug through the pile, searching for the pair of blue jeans that fit just right. Not too tight. Not too loose. Meg sighed when she found her favorite Wranglers. She tugged on the faded jeans and buttoned up her scarlet flannel shirt. The 45 ended. Meg lifted the needle, gently placing it on the edge of the 45. One more listen before school. She sang out—out of key yet rocking to the music as she tucked in her shirt, cinched her belt, and set her cowboy hat squarely on her head. She glanced at the oval mirror on her desk. Wisps of straight dark hair framed her face. *Good enough*, she thought. *Fancy clothes don't mean anything anyhow—it's your brains and heart that count.*

The January air was nippy on Meg's mile walk to school, but not as cold as it got back in Bison Gap. Heck, she didn't even need gloves here in Kentucky. *They call this winter*, Meg chuckled to herself, remembering the twenty below days in Montana. They didn't even cancel school in Montana because of winter weather. They'd all just add extra layers of clothes and go about their days. Folks were tougher out west.

Shiny Cadillacs and station wagons rumbled down the street

toward the school. Not a pickup truck in sight. Approaching the high school, Meg saw kids pour out of yellow school buses. They were all talking and laughing with one another. She sighed, remembering her old school, a friendly place where she knew everyone and their brothers and sisters, too. Here she knew not a soul. Why did her father have to go and take a new job? In Kentucky of all places?

"Hey! Move it, redneck!" a boy in plaid trousers and a turtleneck yelled at her as he ran into her. Startled by his attitude, Meg raised her middle finger and flicked him off. He didn't see her sign language. "Jerk," she spat at him. She pulled her hat down lower over her forehead, hoping to hide from the gaggle of teens running in all directions. She'd need to find the guidance office but she wasn't going to ask anyone for help. She'd find it herself.

Entering the building, Meg dodged girls giggling by their lockers, spritzing on perfume and applying apple-red Revlon lipstick. Guys in letterman jackets gathered around the drinking fountains, joshing with each other, and winking at the girls. Meg checked to make sure her fly was zipped. As she looked up, she spotted signs high on the wall.

Gym

Library

Cafeteria

Main Office

Guidance Office

Guidance, she thought, *precisely what I need*. She edged her way through the crowd, heading toward the guidance office as the first bell rang. Students dashed in all directions, anxious not to be late to class. Within twenty seconds, Meg found herself all alone in the hallway. "That's more like it. Now I've got peace and quiet. Reminds me of home," she said.

The secretary in the guidance office had blue-grey hair piled high on her head. She twiddled a string of pearls around her neck as she held the telephone receiver to her ear. "Yes, sir, I will see to it that we request those transcripts straight away. Um-hmm. Thank you." She hung up the phone. Raising her eyes to Meg, the secretary asked, "What can I help you with, honey?" Her Southern accent sounded breathy and syrupy-sweet to Meg. Was this woman for real or had she stumbled into a re-creation of *Gone with the Wind*?

"I'm uh new here. I uh need to sign up for classes." Meg took her hat off and held it respectfully behind her back.

The secretary looked her up and down. "Are you now?"

"Uh-huh, I mean, uh yes, ma'am."

"What's your name?"

"Meg Murphy." She cleared her throat. "My mother mailed in my new student paperwork a few days ago."

"Well, Meg Murphy, what grade are you in and where are you from? Not Can-tucky, I'm guessing." The blue-haired lady thumbed through a tall stack of manila folders, whispering "Murphy" to herself.

"Ninth grade. Bison Gap, Montana. Ma'am."

The syrupy woman shook her head, "My, my, my. You are a long way from Montana. What brings you here?"

"My dad got a promotion—at the bank—he's vice president now—so we had to move…"

5

Before she could finish explaining, the secretary exclaimed, "Oh! You! I heard all about your daddy. A newcomer. Quite the fella at the main branch…my, you are not quite what I expected to see and all…mmm…" The woman eyed Meg's faded jeans again before adding, "Well, I'm sure you'll find other suitable clothes to wear—after you get through unpacking. Always nice to have more upstanding citizens in this here town."

The secretary opened a manila folder with "Megan Murphy" printed at the top, scribbled a few words on a slip of paper, then looked up at her. "Say, you're also related to Doc and Louise, aren't you?"

Meg nodded. The woman's tone had gone from cool skepticism to warm welcome in a span of ten seconds. *People were weird around here*, she thought. "They're my uncle and aunt." *Although I don't hardly know them.*

"Your cousin Tuck goes to school here. I'll call him out of class. He'll show you to your homeroom."

Meg hadn't actually met Tuck yet. Her family had only moved to town three days prior. They'd barely unpacked, let alone had a family reunion. Her dad's brother, Uncle Doc, had left Montana years before Meg was born. He went east for vet school. After graduating, he met Louise, married her, and set up home with her in Kentucky. Tuck was technically a cousin by marriage only—not blood—he was Aunt Louise's sister's kid. So was he really a cousin at all? Meg rubbed her forehead. *Who cares?* She thought. *He's about my age. It beats hanging around with my mother.*

A lanky red-haired boy sauntered into the guidance office.

"Tucker! Your cousin Meg is ready to start school here," the syrupy secretary sang out to the boy. Meg noted how the woman's eyes danced when she spoke to Tuck. He must be well-liked at the school.

"Hey, there," Tuck said, extending his hand for a shake. "Nice costume, cowgirl."

Meg's initial smile faded. "It's not a costume."

"Oh, sorry," he said. "We cool?"

Meg bit her lower lip, thinking about Tuck's question. He was family by law after all. Even though he, too, was a perfect stranger. She decided to forgive him for his minor transgression. "Sure. We cool."

"Tucker, will you please show Meg where her homeroom class is? She has Mrs. Parker." The secretary handed Meg her class schedule.

"Sure thing, Mrs. Gee. Sure thing," Tuck winked at the secretary. He turned to Meg, "Follow me, Mrs. Parker HATES tardies and you are clearly tardy." Tuck giggled at some secret joke to himself.

Tuck led her through a maze of hallways, pointing out the lunchroom and the gym.

"Here we are, Mrs. Parker's room. Have fun. See ya later, cousin."

"Yeah, thanks," Meg answered as Tuck trotted down the hall, heading back to his own homeroom, all easy-breezy confidence. Meg was stunned that Tuck offered only small talk. He didn't seem glad to meet her— being that they were family and all. Maybe that'll change outside of school.

As she opened the classroom door, she saw a round woman with jet-black hair at the chalkboard. The teacher stopped her lecture. "Who might you be?" she said dryly to Meg.

"I'm new here." Meg turned bright red as thirty sets of eyes bored into her. She handed Mrs. Parker her schedule to prove she did indeed belong there.

Lowering her bi-focal glasses onto her face, Mrs. Parker studied the slip of paper then studied Meg. "Welcome to class, Megan Murphy. In Kentucky, we begin school on time. You may take your seat right here in the front row." Mrs. Parker motioned toward the empty seat closest to the teacher's desk.

Meg obliged and sat down. Homeroom period was intended for daily announcements and reminders. Clearly a methodical person, Mrs. Parker returned her attention to the chalkboard and listed the week's upcoming events: Choir Tryout on Tuesday at 3:30 p.m., Band Concert on Wednesday 7:00 p.m., Winter Social Dance on Friday at 6:00 p.m. "Ladies and gentlemen," Mrs. Parker said. "Please be aware that appropriate dress is required for all school functions." She paused, glaring at Meg. "Ladies, skirts and hose. Gentlemen, slacks and a tie."

Meg glanced over her shoulder, evaluating the other students in the room. They didn't seem fazed by Mrs. Parker's comment on the dress code. Talk about stuffy.

The school bell rattled the silence. Students gathered their books and bustled to their first period classrooms. Meg trailed behind, reading her schedule and the map of the school. Algebra next. Then English, followed by American history, lunch, home economics, earth science, and choir. *Choir! What the?* She had never sung in public in all her life. There had to be some mistake somewhere. Fighting back panic, Meg clutched her notebook to her chest tighter. *Breathe*, she told herself, *just breathe. It's probably a typo.*

By lunchtime, she had already acquired a full night of homework. Her mind reeled from all of the new-to-school information and names to remember. She found her locker next to the cafeteria. After fumbling with the combination lock, she dumped her books into the locker, and slumped back up against it. *If I start walking now, could I make it back to Montana before anyone notices that I'm gone?*

"Howdy, cowpoke!" a familiar enough voice called out. Meg opened her eyes. Tuck. A group of girls giggled at Tuck as he walked by. He waved and gave them his customary wink. *A ladies man*, Meg thought, *great, just great.*

"Where did you park your horse?" Tuck teased her.

Her face clouded over as girls continued to gawk at them.

"Well? Where is he?"

"I had to sell him before we moved." Meg thought of her chestnut gelding, Buckwheat. She had gotten him at auction for a song, practically. The auctioneer had whispered down to her from his booth, and advised her against purchasing him, warning her that the horse was "circling the drain." Yet Meg had nursed Buckwheat back to health, and she'd gone on to make him a fine trail horse. When Dad had told her to sell Buckwheat before the move, Meg had kicked and screamed and cried. She pleaded with him to let her bring Buckwheat out to Kentucky. He'd refused. "Starting a new life" obviously meant leaving loved ones behind. Before she knew it, her father sold Buckwheat to a tourist trail riding operation down by the Stillwater River. Her mother had only patted Meg's head as she cried when the horse trailer hauled Buckwheat away and said, "There, there. You will make new friends in Kentucky." *As if.*

Meg wiped a tear from her eye and looked away from Tuck.
Tuck grew quiet. "Oh."

He seemed so insensitive, so clueless. "Yeah. Oh," she replied.

"Hey, I didn't know you really had a horse. Most kids here don't."

"I'm not most kids."

"I'd say you're not. Hey, sit with me at lunch. You don't want to eat alone, do you?" It was a peace offering of sorts.

"No, thanks. I like to be by myself." She didn't care for his attitude.

She got in the lunch line and then paid for her grilled cheese sandwich and tomato soup. Leaving the line, she navigated through the rows of white Formica topped tables. Reality hit her like a thunderstorm. A small bead of sweat formed under her armpits. She did not know a soul—aside from Tuck. Nobody even looked up or smiled as she wound her way through swarms of students. She glanced over her shoulder. Other students spilled out of the lunch line, waving to their friends. *There's the Young Politicians table*, Meg chuckled to herself. The girls wore mauve and pastel shirtwaist dresses. The guys wore tweed. Not a one in cowboy boots or flannel shirt. *Not a one*. They kinda reminded her of her parents. *What a load of fun.*

She had two options. Her first: Sit at a table near the principal's office. A few rag-tag kids sat there. Their heads were slumped down over their books. They looked nerdy but harmless enough. The other option: Carry her lunch tray to the bathroom and eat lunch in a stall. That might not be a bad option. She wouldn't have to deal with putting herself out there. That was for sure. Could she do it for the whole year? Maybe, although the smell of Pine Sol cleaner might make her nauseous. Probably cause her to lose her appetite. Maybe the bathroom option wasn't so brilliant after all. Maybe she could go talk to the blue-haired secretary and ask for an extra class or study hall instead of lunch. But, for today, the bathroom seemed like the best plan.

At the table nearest the bathroom, a frizzy-haired girl with wide, round glasses looked up just as Meg was about to stroll into the girls' restroom with her lunch tray. "You want to sit here?" the girl asked.

Meg, trying to recover from her dining-in-the restroom plan, replied with a feigned causal-sounding, "Sure."

With that, the owlish girl buried her head back in her book.

Even seated at the table with the girl, Meg felt invisible. If she were to just spontaneously combust—*Poof*—not a soul at the nerd table would even notice. Her head would still be buried in her textbook. Tuck certainly wouldn't notice nor care. Meg chewed her sandwich, rolling the gooey American cheese across her tongue, savoring the creamy, comforting saltiness. The sandwich reminded her of winters in Montana. The nights when her mom would make tomato soup with elbow noodles and cook up buttery grilled cheese sandwiches. Those nights when she felt as if she were in a safe, warm nest. Away from the blowing snowstorms outside.

"You're in my seat." Looking down at Meg was a mouse-faced girl holding a tray of dill pickles, chocolate pudding, and a Twinkie.

Distracted by the unusual cuisine, Meg fumbled. "Uh okay." She slid her lunch tray to the empty seat to her left and hopped over a stool. "Didn't mean to. Sorry."

The mouse-faced girl plopped herself down next to Meg and the owlish girl. She half smiled at the girl and puzzled over such a disgusting choice of food for lunch. Dill pickles certainly didn't count as vegetables.

The mouse-girl slid her tray closer to Meg. "Want some?"

Meg waved the food away. "No. Thanks. I'm allergic to pickles."

Mouse-girl's eyes about popped out of their sockets. "For real?"

Entertained by the dire alarm she caused in this girl, she toyed with her. "For real. Like trip to the ER real."

"Do you have any symptoms if I just sit by you…or…"

Meg smirked at the girl's earnest concern. "I'm just playing. Nobody's allergic to pickles."

"Oh, thank god," the girl sighed. "There for a minute I didn't think we could be friends—I'd never give up pickles. Not for anyone." She let out a flute-like giggle.

The girl leaned close enough so Meg could smell sour dill pickles on her breath. "You new here?" She smiled, revealing a slice of dill pickle stuck in her teeth.

"You got a…" Meg pointed to her own tooth, "piece stuck."

The girl giggled again and wiggled the pickle slice free with her finger. She wiped her fingers on the napkin and extended her hand to Meg for a handshake. "Sarah."

"Meg."

In between darty bites of her Twinkie and her dill pickles, Sarah prattled on about the teachers, especially her favorite

12

teacher, Mrs. Meeker, and the science lab. Sarah spoke, and even moved like a mouse, scurrying from subject to subject.

"You should come with us after school. Right, Eliza?" Sarah slapped owl-girl Eliza on the arm.

Eliza's head jerked up from her book. "Uh, yeah sure."

Sarah went on, "Eliza studies all the time. She wants to be a big shot doctor."

"Chiropractor," Eliza corrected Sarah.

Meg arched an eyebrow. *Not exactly big shot.* Eliza caught Meg's snarky expression.

"Chiropractors are the first line of defense against needless pain and suffering," Eliza pointed out.

"I think orthodontists make more money," Meg snapped, slightly irritated at Eliza's holier-than-thou tone.

"Anyway," Sarah added to diffuse the tension, "Mrs. Meeker has a science club of sorts. You can be part of it. If you want."

"Yeah, thanks. It sounds fun." Meg smiled at Sarah, relieved that these two girls were serious science nerds. "Maybe tomorrow."

Sarah's smile fell. "Sure. Yeah. I get it."

"Get what?"

"I heard you're Tuck's cousin." Sarah gestured towards Tuck who was quite obviously flirting with a preppy girl in a letterman jacket. He had a strand of the girl's hair curled around his fingers. She, meanwhile, cast an adoring, wide-eyed gaze his way.

Meg wrinkled her nose at the thought. "Hardly." Not wanting to hurt Sarah's feelings, Meg added, "I got to let my folks know. Okay?"

"Oh, right. Sure thing," Sarah said.

"Howdeeee!" Tuck called to Meg as he strode toward their table. The girl in the letterman jacket held onto his arm as if she had just caught a prize-winning trout. He stopped at their table and leaned over the girls. "Looks like you're fitting right in." Tuck winked at Meg and sauntered away as if he owned the place.

"Good God," Meg muttered. "What a jerk."

"Can you say that about family?" Sarah asked. "It doesn't seem respectful."

"Yeah. It *should* be said about family. Especially by family. Look, he's only sort of my cousin. What I mean is, he's my cousin. Kind of. By marriage."

"He's one of the most popular guys in school. Everyone *loves* him," Eliza said.

"I can tell. He's fantastic, isn't he?" Meg said, irritated at the casual insults Tuck seemed to lob her way every chance he got.

"He is kinda cute. Which gives him a free pass to be a jerk," Sarah added.

"Not a very feminist thing to say," Eliza pointed out.

Eliza's sharp wit caught Meg off guard. She giggled into the back of her hand. Her eyes met Eliza's droll expression. "Problem?" Eliza asked.

"Oh no. Not at all." Meg answered.

"I make no apologies." Eliza pushed her shoulders back.

"Well, I like your style," Meg smiled at her new friends. Maybe Kentucky wouldn't be so bad after all.

The rest of the school day passed by. Choir class was pure torture. The teacher, Mr. Pratt, did not warmly welcome Meg to the group, especially when he heard her retch out "America the

14

Beautiful." Meg winced when she recalled his critique of her non-existent musical skills. "Like a dying feline," to be precise. Most of the kids in school didn't even bother to strike up a conversation with her. Yet at every break between classes, Tuck would stride through the halls, and flirt with girls, making himself the center of attention. Meg couldn't help but think, *Ain't I lucky?*

CHAPTER 2
Out of Sorts

Meg set the dinner table, carefully arranging the fine china and folding the napkins. Since moving to the South, Mom insisted on setting the table—properly—every evening. Back home in Montana, the fine china used to only come out for Thanksgiving, Christmas, and Easter.

"Meg, dear, go pour yourself a glass of milk for dinner," Mom said as she set a steaming platter of fried chicken on the dining room table.

Dad came downstairs, changed from his business suit to his golf pants and shirt. "MMM. Smells delicious, Suzanne." He sat at the head of the table.

As Mom dished out the chicken, she chirped to her almost picture-perfect family, "How was your first day of school, Meggie?"

Meg shrugged. "All right, I guess."

"All right? What's that supposed to mean?"

"It means all right. Nothing spectacular."

Mom sighed and rested her hands in her lap. "Did you make any friends?"

In between mouthfuls of fried chicken, Meg answered with a casual, "Uh-huh."

"Who are they? Anyone important?" Mom asked her.

"Nope."

Frowning over her chicken breast, Mom said, "Try to get in with the right people here. No more rough neck rodeo kids with beat-up pickup trucks."

"Seriously, Mother," Meg shot back, "No one here even knows what a rodeo is."

"Megan, don't sass back to your mother," Dad said. "You need to put yourself with kids from good families who will make something of themselves."

"Dad," Meg interrupted, "I…"

"Megan, you heard me. Fresh start. New you. Keep your grades up."

To signal that the item was not up for discussion any longer, Dad picked up his newspaper, fanning it so Meg could not see his face. The headline however read: *Nixon Set to Address Nation about Vietnam.*

Silence blanketed the rest of the meal. *Typical*, Meg thought, *typical*. They want a perfect, obedient daughter. A daughter who looks good in person and on paper. Don't they remember where we came from? A town that had more cows than people. A town where the rodeo was the event of the season. A town where it was A-OK to wear faded-out work clothes because work—real, hard, physical work—was something to be proud of.…Who were these people sitting across the table? Mom joined the Bridge Club and Dad is drinking Scotch at a country club. The alien mother ship must have zoomed down and sucked up her real parents and replaced them with alien imposters. Aliens who wanted to appear as all-American as apple pie.

The telephone rang. "I'll get it," Meg shouted, jumping up from the dining room table, sloshing the milk in her glass, and spilling it onto the table. Answering the telephone, she said, "The Murphy residence. May I help you?" Meg rarely answered the phone like that but she adopted her Miss Manners tone just to irritate Mom a smidge more. She shot a smirk at her and then sweetly sang out, "Dad, it's for you."

On their end of the line, all Meg could hear was Dad saying, "Oh, yes, we would love to. Thank you for the invitation."

"Who was that, dear?" Mom asked after he hung up.

"Louise. She wants to welcome us to town by having us over tomorrow night."

"That sounds lovely," Mom purred and then glared at Meg, "You WILL wash up and look presentable."

Meg let out a "hmpfh," that sounded like a noise from a horse.

Later that evening, as Meg finished her algebra homework, she heard her parents' muffled voices coming from their bedroom. Hoping to catch their conversation, Meg placed her ear against the wall.

Mom: *She needs finishing school.*

Dad: *She is rough around the edges.*

Mom: *Rough? She is impossible. Look at her. She will never fit in here. She looks like a tomboy, all scruffy.*

Dad: *Take her shopping. Buy her a few nice outfits.*

Mom: *Shopping?!!? It will take more than that.*

Dad: Radio silence.

Mom: *Honestly, you are vice president of a bank. You can't have a daughter looking all ragged and ranchy. What will people say about us? That we don't train our daughter on how to be a nice young lady? That we look like white trash?*

Meg kicked the wall with her boot. "I can hear you," she yelled at the wall. Silence, followed by muffled whisperings.

Meg threw the algebra textbook off her desk. She pulled her scrapbook out from under her bed. Page after page she'd filled with photos of Buckwheat. Her blue ribbon from the summer's AQHA horse show was on the last page. Her fingers lingered over the embossed gold lettering on the ribbon. A teardrop fell on the page.

CHAPTER 3

Meet the Family

Meg didn't *dress* for dinner. *Heck with them*, she thought. *I remember where I come from.* Mom, grumbling about proper etiquette, carried a pineapple upside down cake to the car. "Stop dawdling. We can't be late for dinner."

Meg gave her mother a scowl and dutifully climbed into the backseat. Dad navigated the station wagon across town, meandering through the tidy residential streets. He hummed softly to himself.

As they pulled the station wagon into Uncle Doc and Aunt Louise's driveway, Mom whispered, "Their house is smaller than I expected."

Dad, turning off the ignition, said, "They don't need much space with no children."

Mom sighed, "Poor dears."

"His practice takes up all their time anyhow."

Mom tssk-tskked in disapproval. "A veterinarian really needs to be a fixture in the community." Mom slid out of the car, balancing the cake as Dad went up and rang the doorbell.

Meg couldn't believe how high and mighty her mother sounded. Who did she think she was? It was like Mom had forgotten their past. The years of scrimping and saving. The thrift stores for blue jeans and boots. The winters where Dad took extra work driving a snow plow to help make ends meet. With this promotion, their lives had changed. But beyond the money, it didn't seem like for the better.

"Meg," Mom hissed, "stop slouching."

The third time Dad rang the doorbell, a tall, tanned woman swung open the front door. She had on a t-shirt and blue jeans. "Hi there!" she smiled, her eyes crinkled at the corners. She wrapped Dad in a hug, followed by Mom, and Meg. "Let me help you carry that. Come on in," the woman said.

A man's baritone voice came from the kitchen. "Need a hand, Louise?"

"No thanks, hon. Keep on cooking." Aunt Louise answered. Her eyes twinkled. "Doc likes to cook every once in a while. It smells like he burnt down the house." Meg was surprised that Aunt Louise didn't seem angry or put out about the smell of burning meat that was wafting through her home. "Have a seat by the fire. Care for a Bourbon? A soda?"

"Milk for Meg," Mom said in a clipped monotone. "Soda water for me. Please."

"I'll take a Bourbon," Dad said as he stretched back in the recliner, like a lazy old house cat who had just been well fed.

Aunt Louise came back with drinks, followed by Uncle Doc. He looked no-nonsense, in a homespun kind of way. Not like a fancy doctor at all. He had a chipped plate loaded with crispy hot dogs and buns. Aunt Louise pulled a stack of paper plates out from the cupboard. Uncle Doc sat the food on the coffee table. Meg could see her mother visibly recoil at the informality of the occasion. "Make yourselves at home," Aunt Louise said, smiling at her extended family.

Meg relaxed on the sofa, savoring the hot dog and the casual laughter coming from her Uncle Doc and Aunt Louise as they reminisced about their dating days. *Uncle Doc and Aunt Louise*, Meg smiled to herself, *look like they fell right off the turnip truck. I like them. They are about perfect.*

Doc looked at his brother. "I can't believe you and Suzanne ever left Montana."

Dad cleared his throat. "We needed a change of scenery. A fresh start." He took a sip of his Bourbon. "The job offer was too good to pass up."

Aunt Louise reached out to Mom, touching the top of her hand as lightly as a bird landing on a branch. "How are you doing?" Meg noticed that Aunt Louise's merry expression turned to one of deep concern and worry. "It is a big move for the three of you."

"Yes, yes, it is," Mom replied as stiff as a corpse.

"Suzanne, hon, we are family. Don't be all formal with me," Louise said.

Mom smoothed her hair behind her ears. "Well, that's behind us now."

Louise smiled tenderly, "Have it your way. But if you ever want to talk, I'm here for you."

The room went silent as if Aunt Louise had crossed the border between East and West Germany and she was in enemy territory.

"We are doing fine, just fine, Louise. Don't you worry about us," Dad said.

Yeah, right, Meg thought. *Fine, super fine. My parents have had frontal lobotomies and have lost their minds. Mom wears real pearls now for Chrissakes!*

Louise narrowed her eyes and studied the three Murphys. "You okay after the baby?"

Baby? What baby? Meg wondered. Meg was an only child. Aunt Louise must have Mom confused with someone else in the family.

Mom shot Meg a sideways glance and, meeting Louise's eyes again, answered, "Yes, fine. Thank you. Can I help you clean up?" Mom stood up, smoothed the wrinkles from her dress, and went out to the kitchen. Aunt Louise followed her. Meg caught a muffled "I'm so sorry...I thought you told her." It sounded like Aunt Louise's voice. *What had happened to Mom and a baby?* Thoughts ricocheted around in Meg's mind. Then two and two came together. Mom had been pregnant and miscarried. *My God*, Meg thought, *why didn't they tell me?*

Uncle Doc and Dad were quiet. Meg thumbed through a newspaper on the end table, pretending to mind her own business and tamp down her hurt.

Then Doc said, "We are more than glad to have the three of you out here. Louise has family scattered all over the state, but for me, well, I missed you, brother." Uncle Doc slapped Dad's back. "I'm glad it's working out."

"The money is good. The school is top-notch. Suzanne is making an effort to fit in and make friends. She's getting out of the house. Being social." Dad took a sip of Bourbon. "New year, new start."

"I'll drink to that," Doc said.

"Starting over sucks," Meg said.

"It is what you make of it," Dad said as he lifted the Bourbon to his lips again.

Doc replied, "For what it's worth, kiddo, I think you will be okay. Trust me on this one."

By nine o'clock, they were ready to call it a night. The winter air was brisk as the Murphys left. Aunt Louise, standing in the doorway of her home, wrapped Meg in a bear hug. "Don't be a stranger. Come over anytime you need to."

"I will. Thank you, Aunt Louise."

"Anytime," Uncle Doc piped in. "Although I'm not usually done with the horses until about six o'clock. But any time after that, kiddo, anytime. You are family."

Horses? Meg's attention was piqued.

"Thank you for a lovely evening," Mom said, as if intentionally diverting Meg's attention away from the word *horses*, and shooed her toward the car.

Meg stayed up later than usual that evening. She had an English paper to draft for homework. Mom had already put cold cream on her face and retired to bed. Just Dad sat downstairs, reading the newspaper.

"Hey, Dad."

"Yes?"

"What did Doc mean about horses?"

"He has rounds to finish."

"Rounds?"

Dad rubbed his eyes. "He's a veterinarian, Meg. He has horse patients."

A gear shifted in Meg's brain. *Horse patients.* All this time, she'd just thought Doc was a common old veterinarian, doing all the common old household dogs and cats and parakeets and hamsters. Horses? Horses were a different story altogether.

Dad looked up from his newspaper, waiting for Meg to respond.

When she didn't, he made a contented little sound and went back to reading his paper.

Meg did her best to concentrate on writing her English report but horses galloped through her mind instead.

CHAPTER 4

A Proposal

A month into Meg's "fresh start" in Kentucky, she'd made all of two friends: Eliza and Sarah. Tuck hardly counted. He was simply an obnoxious shirttail relative. Although Meg had always told herself that everything in life revolved around quality not quantity, she couldn't shake the sinking feeling that folks in Kentucky didn't even see her. Like she was a phantom drifting through the school hallways. Even the teachers didn't pay her any mind. On the first day, they'd all taken stock of her appearance. Too rough. Too Western. Too cowgirly. After that initial evaluation, she was a non-entity to practically everyone. Back home, she had been surrounded by friends and relatives. They'd all grown up together, attended church together, football games, rodeos, and everyone knew everyone's business. There were no strangers back in Bison Gap. Moving to Kentucky had changed all of that. Meg was the stranger. She felt unsettled. Cast off like a piece of driftwood on the Yellowstone River.

She'd tried to voice this to Eliza and Sarah at lunch. They had shrugged it off. Eliza, nonchalantly replied, "They only pay attention to the jocks or the rich kids. Nobody else matters."

"We're not poor," Meg had tried, for once, to speak on behalf of her parents.

"Maybe not, but your family hasn't lived here for two hundred years and you dress like a farmer."

Sarah, the optimist, added, "Wait until college. My brother goes to OSU and he says it is way better than high school."

Meg had trudged home that day, terribly homesick for her old school and friends. They used to hang out at the river on the weekends, fishing or playing football. Or, they'd go out riding along the rimrocks, down by the train tracks. Their horses gingerly picking their way across the tracks and winding their way up through the sandstone hills west of town. Everyone looking out for one another. Everyone enjoying sound horses and good friends. Meg wanted to call them or write letters but she figured it was useless since she'd never see them again. Besides, she didn't want any of them to find out just how miserable she was. They'd only remind her that the grass isn't always greener on the other side. And they'd tell her that she should have never left Montana. As if she had any control over that decision.

As Meg walked up her driveway, she saw Aunt Louise's truck. Inside, she found Aunt Louise thumbing through a *Better Homes and Garden* magazine.

"Howdy, girl," Aunt Louise said. "How was school?"

Meg dropped her books on the table. "Fine."

"Fine, huh. Just fine. Sounds like a pretty dry way to go through life to me, being *fine*."

Meg went to the kitchen. "Where's my mom?"

"Oh, she got invited to the Garden Club. She just couldn't refuse," Aunt Louise giggled, then apologized, "I'm sorry. That was disrespectful."

"The Garden Club. Oh boy." Meg undid her ponytail and ran

her fingers through her hair, as if she could scratch the lackluster school day away. "When will she be home?"

"Oh, five-ish, I'm sure. But until then, you got me, kid, to entertain you."

"I don't need a babysitter."

"I know. But your mom said you've been looking lonely. You hungry?"

"Starving."

"Good. Let's go grab burgers and take 'em out to Doc." Aunt Louise sprung from the sofa, grabbed her truck keys, and was out the door in a fraction of a second. "Come on, kid. I'm craving a cheeseburger like there's no tomorrow."

They stopped at the Burger Dive and ordered three cheeseburgers and three chocolate milkshakes to go. The smell of fresh, greasy burgers filled the cab of the truck. Meg's stomach growled.

"We'll be there in a flash," Aunt Louise laughed. "Then we can all eat together."

"There" turned out to be a magnificent horse farm, rows of white barns spread out on rolling hills and trimmed with white fences. Meg's breath caught in her throat.

"Doc's in the back barn, checking the mares," said Aunt Louise as she parked the truck near the hay shed. "It'll probably be a late night for him. Let's see if we can entice him to take an early dinner break with us."

Aunt Louise led Meg through a well-kept facility. Floors were swept. Manure was shoveled. A real professional place, all business. Meg counted twenty horses in the stalls they walked past. All glossy and well-conditioned. Brass name plates on the stall doors. Aunt Louise smiled at Meg, "Gorgeous, aren't they?"

The scent of alfalfa. Of earth. Of leather. The gentle sound of rustling grain in bins. A horse's contented nicker. Meg felt, at once, at home and homesick. A tear slid down her cheek.

"Hey, Doc said you had a horse back home."

Meg trembled, remembering Buckwheat. "I did."

"It's hard to say good-bye to a good one, isn't it?"

Meg tried to stifle her tears, not wanting to look like a baby in front of her aunt.

"You got to love them while you have them," Aunt Louise said. "Nothing is forever. Right?"

Meg could think of nothing to say. Instead she silently prayed that her Buckwheat was alive and happy along the Stillwater River, being a good trail horse for the tourists, not nipping at the kids.

"Ladies!" Doc called out from the last stall. "I hear ya. But I can't see ya. I'm over here. With Shiloh."

They found Doc with a stethoscope on a sorrel mare's side. "There, there, mama," he softly said to Shiloh, the mare. "Baby sounds strong." He patted the mare's side and walked out of the stall, closing the door behind him. "Looks like you brought dinner. Let me wash up."

Aunt Louise pulled two tack boxes from the front of the stall. "Have a seat," she said to Meg.

Doc came back, patting his stomach. "I am hungry. Thanks for thinking of me."

Doc recounted the mares he examined while Louise was gone

to pick up Meg. She would make notes on their files when she got back to the office. All of the mares were pregnant. "Most seem to be progressing along nicely. But you can never be 100 percent certain with horses," Doc said.

After the medical details were discussed, Doc leaned into Meg, "Your dad used to be quite the reiner in his day. Believe that? Now he's a laced up banker. Ha ha! Who would have ever predicted that one?"

Meg had heard stories about Doc and her dad. Most folks had said they both could have gone pro, if they wanted to.

"Must have been hard on him to sell your home place," Doc added quietly.

"Hardly. He got the job offer and out we went. No looking back." Meg scratched at the hole in the knee of her blue jeans. "He doesn't miss it at all."

"Hey, now. Your father wanted to see your mother happy. Too many bad memories for her." Doc went on, "Besides, he's always wanted to make a name for himself. Let's face it, that wasn't going to happen out there. He needed to move to a bigger region, a bigger bank."

Meg half muttered, "Whatever. They seemed happy enough."

Aunt Louise placed her hand on Meg's knee, stopping her from picking at her blue jeans. "There's a lot your parents don't tell you. Try to understand."

"I lost my best friend because of my parents. They don't give two shakes about that. Like Buckwheat was replaceable. Disposable."

It was Doc who tried to soothe Meg this time, "None of

them are replaceable. None of 'em. But you carry on by counting your blessings and doing right by the new ones who come into your life, sweetheart. It ain't easy. Never is."

Meg shook her head. "I hate them. Hate them for it." Meg got up to throw her cheeseburger wrapper away. "They'd probably throw me away in a heartbeat, too."

"Oh, honey, no. They wouldn't. Don't talk like that," Aunt Louise attempted to settle Meg down. "It's just, it's just that things happen and change a family. They are trying to do their best. Give them a chance."

"Why should I? They moved me here. Here to a school filled with nobody like me. I have two friends. Count them. One, two. I could fall off the face of the Earth and only those two people would notice." Meg kicked at the tack box, startling the sleeping horses with the loud thud of her boot.

Doc narrowed his eyes, "What do you mean, 'nobody like you'?"

Using her hands, Meg motioned them down her body. "Nobody real. Nobody country. All these kids look like they stepped out of a fashion magazine. Well scrubbed. It's like I'm surrounded by an entire town filled with the Young Bankers of America Club."

Aunt Louise let out a guffaw. "Honey," she said, "that's cuz you're going to school in Lexington. All *those* kids belong to doctors and lawyers. Come on over to where we live in Paris— with the working people. Most of us work in the horse business."

Meg's forehead wrinkled in surprise.

"Your aunt is right. Hasn't your father taken you for a drive

31

through the country? To see the horse farms?"

"No." She didn't know what Doc was talking about. Dad had driven her past the Country Club, the golf course, the mansions, fancy department stores, but not out toward any farms.

"Well, he should have. That's how most of us make our living. Sweetheart, you landed in a little piece of Thoroughbred heaven here." Doc waved his arms out to the side. "This is one of many fine facilities. You're a horse gal. I think you'll fit right in."

Meg's anger melted into disbelief. "Truly?"

"Truly," Louise and Doc answered in unison.

"Nothing will ever be able to replace the love you had for your first horse but…" Aunt Louise paused, choosing her words carefully, "but, we'd sure like to spend time with you. Get to know you."

Doc added, "Besides, foaling season will be here in a month or two. I could always use extra hands. If you're at all interested?"

Without hesitation, Meg jumped at Doc's offer. "Thank you," she said as she wrapped her arms around her uncle's neck. "Thank you."

"Don't thank me just yet," he laughed. "It is a lot of work, young lady."

"I ain't afraid of hard work. I prefer it," Meg said, remembering her time with Buckwheat, shoveling his stall, loading hay, and hauling water. Her heart swelled with memories. Maybe Kentucky wouldn't be so bad, after all.

CHAPTER 5

Hello, World!

Claiborne Farm, Paris, Kentucky

April 17, 1972

9:42 p.m.

"Feel for the front legs," Doc said, "Help her out."

Meg wrapped her fingers around the slick sack and felt around for the foal's hooves.

"Got 'em." Meg squatted back on her haunches.

"Pull," Doc said. "But pull slow and steady. And stop when I say stop."

Doc watched the mare's breathing and saw her side heave. A contraction.

"Now pull."

Meg pulled.

"Wait," Doc whispered. Doc's hands were on the mare's face. The mare, Shenanigans, was sweaty and lying on her side. The birth of this foal was taking longer than usual.

The mare took another breath. Doc could see her muscles rippling in contractions like waves crossing the ocean.

"Pull now," Doc ordered.

Meg hunkered down on her legs, leaned back, and tugged on the foal's wet legs with all her might.

"Stop."

Meg stopped.

The mare's side heaved again with a contraction.

"Pull."

She pulled the foal's front legs. More of its body slid from its mother.

"Stop."

Meg's arms and back ached. The pungent smell of bodily fluids and alfalfa hay caught in her nose and throat. She felt queasy, on the verge of passing out. She tried to bury her face in her shoulder, to block the smell, to stop the gag reflex.

"You okay?"

Meg swallowed hard. "Yes, sir." Her skin felt cold and clammy.

"Hang in there. A few more contractions and the baby'll be out."

The mare heaved again.

Doc said, "Pull."

As Meg pulled, the foal slid a little farther from its mother's body. The sack around the foal broke. She caught sight of a black nose and long front legs.

"Attagirl, Meggie! You've almost got 'em out," Doc said proudly.

Five more pulls and stops and they had the foal halfway out of the mare.

Then, in one wet gush of fluid and flesh, a jet-black foal slipped from the mare's body.

Meg landed on her rear end in the soft hay. She gazed at the foal's spindly legs and its large dark face. Its ears were pinned back and then twitched forward.

Alive. Thank God. It is alive, Meg wanted to shout from the rafters. Or cry. She didn't know which. She had never been so bone tired before, or so happy. The baby was the most beautiful creature she'd ever seen. All wobbly innocence and charm. As if good things were possible. It was strange this feeling of hopefulness.

Shenanigans, the mare, rolled herself up to turn and study her foal. The sack still clung to the newborn. Mother and baby breathed hard, one resting from a hard delivery, the other adjusting to the crisp spring air and bright lights of the new world.

The foal, turning left then right, smelled for its mother. Its nose touched Shenanigans' right hock. Its ears twitched as it registered its mother's scent.

"Attagirl," Doc said proudly to Shenanigans as he backed away to let her get to her feet.

Shenanigans grunted and heaved herself up. Her grey coat was sweat-soaked but she looked relieved. She turned to her newborn foal and began licking the baby. Her velvet tongue swept across the foal's face, ears, and neck. She whinnied to her baby and nuzzled it. Her tongue swept up and down the length of its body.

The foal lifted its nose up to its mother.

"Nose kisses," Meg chuckled quietly so as not to disturb the moment.

Doc nodded and wiped a tear from his cheek. Even for a seasoned old veterinarian like himself, tender moments still got to him.

"Get on up, little fella," Doc whispered.

The foal quivered.

"Should I help it?" Meg asked. Unsure of how much help to give, she moved cautiously toward the foal.

"Nope. It has got to stand on its own. That's the first lesson in life."

They watched as the wet foal quivered again. Its back legs jerked out. Its head shot forward. Front legs lurched out. Up! The foal was up!

"That's a fella," Doc laughed as the foal wobbled to and fro. It rocked back, looking as if it was going to sit on its rump in the hay. It yanked itself forward, righting its backward momentum. It wobbled to the left and pitched over on its side into the hay.

Doc let out a deep belly laugh. "What a peanut!"

"Is it okay? Did he get hurt?"

Doc laughed more, "He's fine. Ah, no! I mean, she's fine. All new beginnings are a little rocky to start."

A girl! A baby girl.

The foal twitched her ears back in irritation. She stuck her head out and pulled forward with all her might. Up again!

Shenanigans came close, nickered, and nosed her foal, as if checking to be sure all her parts and pieces were there. Satisfied, Shenanigans shifted her attention to the grain bin.

The foal tumbled about the stall, experimenting with her newfound legs.

"You think Mrs. Janney is going to race this one? Or keep her for a brood mare?" Meg asked as she watched the foal teeter about.

Disinfecting his hands with a bar of soap and then rinsing them in a bucket filled with water, Doc shrugged. "It's hard to say so early. Depends on how she grows and if she has fire in her." Doc paused while he dried his hands on a towel and passed the soap to Meg, motioning for her to wash up, too. "Not all of 'em are cut out for racing. Though Shenanigans comes from a long line of speed. Her sire was Native Dancer."

Meg gazed at the jet-black foal, stumbling around the stall, tail twitching, acting annoyed by her body's lack of coordination. "She's a fighter. I can tell."

Doc patted Meg on the back. "Well, kid, I hope so. Now, let's let these two have some peace and quiet."

Doc shoveled the sack and the soiled hay into a wheelbarrow and rolled it out of the stall. Meg slid the stall door shut, latching it securely.

"Get your rest, Mama," Doc said fondly to Shenanigans. "And be good, baby."

Doc put his arm around Meg's shoulders. "Thanks for all your help tonight. She couldn't have done it without you." They walked out of the barn content with a job well done. For once, Meg had nothing to say. She'd worked hard, followed Doc's directions, and helped bring a foal into the world. Everyone was safe and healthy. And Meg couldn't wait to get to know this little sprite of a creature.

CHAPTER 6

Finding a Name

Ten days later, Meg spotted Tuck in the paddock, leaning against the fence. Come to find out, Tuck had been helping out at the vet practice for the past couple of summers. "To lighten the load, a bit," Doc told Meg, when they were busy with foals. Lately, at work, Meg had found she didn't mind Tuck as much as she did in school. His peacocking and flirty attitude toned down around the horse people. Thank goodness.

In the pasture, Shenanigans grazed on the bluegrass while her jet-black foal jumped about like a jackrabbit. Robins flew from tree to tree. Morning. It was Meg's favorite time of day at the barn—before all of the commotion of training sessions. Something about today made her feel playful. Alive.

Sneaking up behind Tuck, she yelled, "Boo!" as she pushed him into the fence. The foal, startled by Meg's loud noise and sudden movement, bolted across the pasture.

"What'd you go and do that for?" Tuck asked, irritated.

Meg giggled. "You looked lost in a daydream and I wanted to shake you out of it."

"Well, you did."

"Oh, stop looking so sore. You can tease me plenty. But you can't take any?"

"What do you want? Don't you have any more feeding to do?"

"Doc wants us to bring these two into the barn for a check-up. I'll help you lead the little gal in." Meg liked to tag along with Doc on his rounds when she could. Otherwise, she earned a little extra spending money helping muck out stalls at Claiborne. Like Tuck, she did everything from feeding and watering the horses to grooming and turn-out duty in the pastures. And, of course, scooping poop. A lot of poop. It was a decent part-time job for folks who loved being around animals as much as she did. She was surprised to find out that Tuck had so willingly signed up to work at Claiborne, too. Tuck had first struck Meg as the type of guy who was all bluster and no work ethic. But maybe she had rushed too fast to judgment. He had helped birth the rest of the foals, right alongside her and Doc. He could work hard when he wanted to, she guessed. Maybe he was growing on her.

Tuck unwrapped the lead ropes from the fence post and tossed the shorter of the two to Meg. "I'll get Mama. You just keep baby close." He walked into the pasture and hooked the lead rope to Shenanigans' halter. She whinnied to the foal. In a rollicking dash, the foal bounded toward Shenanigans.

"Watch out, Meg. That rascal will knock you over to get to her mama."

Sure enough, the black foal barreled toward Meg, skidding to a stop inches away. She snorted a warm dragon's puff of earthy alfalfa breath into Meg's face.

"You are a spitfire, little gal," Meg teased. She didn't shy away from this feisty foal or any other horse.

Taking hold of the other lead rope, she snapped it on the foal's halter. Tuck led the mare back to the barn while Meg followed with the frisky foal, clucking at her to stay in line with her mama.

Nearing the barn, Meg saw the blacksmith, Bruce, pull up in his work truck. Bruce waved to the kids. Tuck turned the corner and led the little family into the barn. Doc, waiting in the alleyway between the rows of stalls, had his thermometer and stethoscope ready.

"Look at this pretty family," Doc said as they walked up to him. "Tuck, you keep mama still. Meg, you keep babe within eyesight of mama. We don't want anyone to panic and hurt themselves."

Doc took Shenanigans' vital signs and made notes in his yellow legal pad. "Your turn, baby girl." Doc motioned for Meg to bring the foal closer to him.

The foal tried to sidestep away from Doc but Meg nudged her toward him, using her body weight and her voice to teach the baby important horse etiquette. When people ask you to do something, you do it—without a fuss.

Doc examined the foal from top to bottom. "She's looking good. And getting real big real fast."

Meg asked, "What's she weigh?"

"I'd say one fifty. Or thereabouts." Doc packed up his medical instruments. "Growing like a weed."

The foal whinnied at Doc, as if laughing with him.

"Looks like she's got a case of foal-heat diarrhea," Doc added. "To be expected, at this age."

"What?"

"Foals get like this. Mama's milk changes and the baby'll get the runs."

Wrinkling her nose, Meg let an "ewww" escape her mouth.

"She needs her rear end washed up," Doc noted, pointing at the foal's hindquarters. "She's got manure all under her tail."

Tuck backed away from the poop-covered bottom. "I gotta go see if Bruce needs a hand getting the horses for shoeing," Tuck stuttered as he turned on his heels and dashed away.

"Figures," said Doc, "That boy never had a strong stomach. He can barely handle the births."

Doc pointed to the wash rack. "Meg, you take the baby's lead rope and follow me. I'll walk mama over."

The dark springy foal bunny-hopped after her mama. Doc clipped Shenanigans' halter to the wash rack post. "Meg, lead baby on in."

Meg clucked her tongue into the roof of her mouth. "Come on, baby girl," she said in a whisper. When the foal's hooves touched the rubber floor mat in the wash rack, she spooked and jumped backwards, in a rear. "Easy girl, just a little rubber mat to keep you from slipping and sliding," she reassured the foal.

"You got her, Meg. Good work," Doc said. "Now, I'll hold her while you turn on the water hose and scrub the poop off her back end."

"With?"

Doc's eyes sparkled. "With your hands, girl."

Meg studied her hands. She'd shoveled plenty of poop—with a *shovel*—but she'd never had to actually *touch* it.

"Test the water. Be sure it ain't too cold. The soap is on the rack. Wet the area down, scrub, then rinse." The foal wiggled away. Doc gathered the foal and wrapped his arms around her neck. "Be

41

soft though. Her skin back there is delicate."

The foal squealed and wriggled again. Doc repositioned himself. By now Doc had the foal in a head lock, to keep her still so she wouldn't hurt herself or one of them. At the sound of the running water, the foal hopped forward, away from the hose. She almost whipped her face into Doc's. "Whoa, girl. Easy." Doc held onto the foal even tighter. "Go on, get it done fast. She's hard to hold still."

Spraying the warm water under the foal's tail certainly didn't settle her down. She tried to jump forward and backward out of Doc's arms. She shook her head fiercely, trying to get as far away from the silly humans as possible. Meg hoped Doc had a tight hold on the foal. She didn't want to get kicked by a hind leg. Meg squirted the liquid soap into her hands and then scrubbed one rear cheek and the other, lifting the caked-on manure off of the little horse with her fingernails. The wet manure ran down the horse's hind legs. Although it looked like chocolate milk, it didn't smell like it. Meg didn't have time to be grossed out. She tried to work fast and soft because Doc was huffing and puffing as he tried to hold the wiry foal.

"How's it looking back there?" Doc panted. "Almost got it all?"

"Almost." Meg rinsed off the foal's backside. "A little left." Meg reached for more soap. "I'm going to wash her one more time." Meg lathered the foal's cheeks faster this time and worked her fingers back and forth over the remaining clumps of manure. "This should do it," she said, reaching for the water hose. She sprayed the foal's rear and the foal shot out of Doc's arms like a giant hopping toad. Doc grabbed the foal's lead rope before she could dart away through the barn.

"Spunky little thing, isn't she?" Doc laughed as he wiped the sweat off his forehead. "She's a lot to hold onto." The foal snorted and tried to pull away from Doc. "Rinse your hands and grab the A&D cream, Meg."

"A&D?"

"Yes, ma'am. Just the stuff for all baby bums. It's on the shelf. Hurry up."

Meg fetched the large round A&D container from the medicine shelf.

"Hey, grab a latex glove, too," Doc shouted from the wash rack. "And put it on your hand."

Nearing the foal's rear, Meg, wearing a blue surgical glove on her right hand, approached the jumpy horse slowly. Doc held the foal as steady as he could. "Smear the ointment all over her— where the manure was—it'll prevent more manure from sticking."

Now he tells me to wear a glove, Meg thought. She realized Doc had given her some kind of test. She dug in and grabbed a thick glob of diaper ointment with her gloved hand. She applied the ointment on the foal, taking care to be tender. Doc twisted around and checked Meg's handiwork.

"Not bad for your first time, kid. Not bad."

She stepped back, smiling. "Never thought I'd ever have to do something like that."

Doc laughed, "Get her and mama back out to the pasture. Let her go play. She was a good girl."

The foal let out a long neigh to her mama and gave her thick, coarse tail a twitch.

"Mrs. Janney is coming to see her in two weeks. I hope she'll be pleased with this young one."

"How could she not be?" she asked. "She's beautiful."

"Beauty does not mean anything for a racehorse. Speed is everything in this business." Doc reminded her.

She took the lead this time with the foal. Doc walked the mare just a stride behind.

"What do you think Mrs. Janney will name her?" Meg asked.

"Fireball."

She shook her head in disagreement. "No way. This foal needs something classy. Like Lynda Carter."

"Who?" Doc asked.

"The actress."

"Wonder Woman?"

Meg smiled, "Yes. Look at this dark-haired beauty. Strong like Wonder Woman."

"You are too much," Doc chuckled as they neared the pasture. "It's all up to Mrs. Janney. Who knows what she'll decide? She's the boss mare."

• • • • •

A confident, stylish woman strolled through the barn, inspecting each horse. Mrs. Barbara Janney, or Bobbi as her close friends called her, renowned equestrienne and horse breeder. Her eagle-sharp eyes missed no detail. When she approached each groom, she asked pointed questions about appetite, exercise regimen, and soundness. Even normally cocky horsemen tensed up when Mrs. Janney grilled them.

Doc, running late from a busy vaccination schedule, hurried down the barn's alley to Mrs. Janney's side. "Morning, ma'am."

"Good morning, Doc. Where is that new filly of mine I've heard so much about?"

"She's out in the nursery pasture with the other broodmares and foals."

"Fresh air and sunshine does the horses good. I don't like to see them cooped up all day. Horses need time to be horses."

"Yes, ma'am. I couldn't agree with you more."

"Take me out to see them, Doc."

They hopped onto a golf cart and sped out to the nursery paddock. The bluegrass sparkled with morning dew. Wild turkeys strutted down the tree-lined lane, not hurrying away from the golf cart.

"Spring is my favorite time of year," Mrs. Janney said. "The earth smells fresh. Young. Anything and everything is possible." She ran her fingers through her hair. "Even I feel young."

They drove across rolling pastures of yearling Thoroughbreds. Bays, chestnuts, sorrels. All well fed and strong. Near the back of the property they came to the nursery pasture. Half a dozen brood mares and foals grazed on the damp grass.

Doc parked the golf cart near the large, grey mare, Shenanigans. Her jet-black filly nursed.

"Okay," Doc said. "There she is."

Mrs. Janney leaned against the fence rail. "My goodness. She is big. You weren't kidding."

"No, ma'am, I rarely kid about horses."

The filly, hearing Mrs. Janney's laugh, stopped nursing, looked at Mrs. Janney, and snorted. The filly sprang toward them. She ran straight to the fence and skidded to a stop in front of them at the rail. Her baby whiskers curled around her mouth. Her long dark ears twitched with curiosity.

"Look at her eyes," Mrs. Janney gasped. "Deep dark pools. And a little star on her forehead."

"She is a beaut."

"An uncommon beauty. And it looks like she's sizing us up and she's ready to take us on."

"There's no fear in this one," Doc said. "She's bold."

Mrs. Janney walked the fence line. The filly trotted alongside her, raising her head high and sniffing the air.

"She moves well. Nice, strong haunches." She stopped and reached out to pet the filly's nose. "I like this one a lot."

"Mrs. Janney, what are your plans for her? Might I ask?"

Mrs. Janney continued to study the filly. "Her mother comes from a swift bloodline, Doc. Native Dancer, the Grey Ghost as he was called, is this filly's grandfather." She paused, lost in thought, "Native Dancer was a legend. He won twenty-one of his twenty-two races, including the Belmont and the Preakness."

"You have high hopes for this filly, Mrs. Janney."

"She's the granddaughter of the wind itself."

The filly sang to her mother and danced off to join her by the watering trough. Mrs. Janney leaned against the fence. She folded her arms across her chest. "Let's give her a year to grow. Then we'll decide."

"Yes, ma'am," Doc replied although he knew Mrs. Janney had

already decided what to do with this youngster. She would be a racer. "Have you thought of a name? I need to get her registered."

"Give me time to think on it, Doc." Mrs. Janney got into the golf cart, ready to head back to the barn. "Stuart flies in from Boston in a few days. I'll bring him by and see what he thinks."

• • • • •

Mrs. Janney led her husband, Stuart, to the pasture. Meg and Tuck were already there, sneaking peppermints to Shenanigans and her still unnamed three-month-old filly. The horses smacked their lips and nickered for more treats.

Mr. Janney, also an expert horseman, smiled in appreciation at the large, strong filly. "Well done, my dear," he said to Mrs. Janney, proud of his wife's breeding strategy.

"Thank you, love. A foal out of Native Dancer's line is bound to be gorgeous." Mrs. Janney reached over the fence and scratched the filly's neck.

Meg and Tuck stood close, careful not to interrupt the Janneys. The owners were always treated like royalty. That was part of running a business. Owners controlled the money; they controlled the big decisions. No questions asked.

"It's time we register the filly and give her a name," Mrs. Janney told them. Meg knew Mrs. Janney liked to name the foals. It was like naming children for her, Doc had said. Today they had two foals to name, a colt and a filly. Their names had to be decided upon so that they could register them in the Jockey Club. This was the first step to becoming a Thoroughbred racehorse.

"That colt over there, what did you want to call him?

Ruffian?" Mr. Janney asked, pointing to a sorrel colt grazing nearby with his mother. "He doesn't look built to be a speedster. I don't think he has the potential to win the big races. Not much of a ruffian, don't you think?"

Mrs. Janney, watching the colt's movements, said, "He's pretty but I think you're right on this one."

Mr. Janney stumbled for words. "Maybe find a name that speaks to his red color not his er um personality?"

"Sell him and focus on training one who can handle the big stakes races," she decided.

The jet-black filly spooked and bolted across the pasture, away from the small gathering of people. Shenanigans trotted away, to stay close to her filly. Mr. Janney, pointing across the pasture at Shenanigans and her filly, said, "Look at that girl. Big and strong. A freak of nature," he laughed.

Tuck started to laugh too until Meg kicked his calf and rolled her eyes. She whispered under her breath, "She's not a freak. And don't disrupt business."

"A freak in a good way, I think," Tuck whispered back. "She's different all right. Like you."

Meg grumbled back at Tuck, "You're one to talk."

Ignoring the teenagers, Mrs. Janney studied Shenanigans' filly. "Yes. I like her. She's got something there."

"Fire," Meg whispered.

"Yes, fire," Mrs. Janney said as if lost in prayer.

Mr. Janney asked, "What does she remind you of? A gladiator? Call her Gladiator."

Mrs. Janney shook her head, "No. No. She's our Ruffian."

"Ruffian? For a girl?" Mr. Janney asked.

"Girls can be ruffians too," she said. "And she's going to South Carolina to train with Frank Whiteley. This filly is going to learn how to be a racehorse."

CHAPTER 7

Goodbye, Mama

October 1972

O n a five-thousand-acre farm, work schedules were important, to say the least. The first Saturday in October was the most stressful time for everyone. Weaning day. The day when all of the foals who were born in March and April would be separated from their mamas. Everyone was expected to work on that day, including the part-timers like Meg and Tuck.

In the barn's office, Meg poured Doc a piping hot cup of coffee. Doc was reviewing charts, checking medical histories, and updating feeding notes. Tuck walked in. His arms were loaded down with baby halters and lead ropes.

"Here you are, Doc. Twelve halters and leads for the babies."

"Thanks, son. You and Meg go hang a set on each of the stall doors in Barn 4. I'll be there in a jif."

They crossed the shed row, walked past three long barns, each filled with world class Thoroughbreds. Barn 4 was painted white with green trim.

"I hope Doc warned you. We're gonna hear more wailing than you'll ever care to remember," Tuck said.

"He did. He said it's constant crying." She paused and put

her hand over her heart. "That crying will do me in for sure."
Doc had told her there was no worse sound in the world than a
spindly-legged colt wailing for its mama. A mama that it would
never see again. Even on that off-chance that it did see her again,
it would never know that she was its mama. The thought of it just
broke Meg's heart. She wished she could've called in sick today.
But with so much work to do, Doc would've fired her for sure.
And she didn't want to get fired. She loved cleaning the horses
and feeding them. She loved their earthy smell and their quirky
personalities. *Horses were better than most people*, Meg thought. No
way would she ever want to lose this job.

She laced the halters on the outside of each stall door. Mares
and foals sniffed at her hands as she went by. She forced a smile to
fight back her tears.

"Hey, no room for softies in this business," scolded Nick
Lotz, the man in charge of breaking Ruffian, as he walked up to
Meg. "If you're gonna get all mushy and sentimental then I'll ask
someone else to do your job. Send you home to your mama."

Meg got rattled, thinking about her own mother's nagging.
She bit down on her quivering lower lip. She remembered a time
when she and her mom had been inseparable. Two peas in a pod,
Dad used to laugh. When did it all change?

"No, sir, er, I mean, yes, sir," Meg wiped her face with the
sleeve of her shirt. What horrible timing. Nick had to come
through the barn and see her about to blubber like a baby.

"Time for these young ones to learn how to work, to be
racehorses." Nick squared his shoulders and placed his hands on
his hips. His face looked gruff, all business, no sentimentality.
"Tuck, boy! You lead out Erin's baby. Meg, you take out

Shenanigans' filly."

Meg slid the stall door open. Shenanigans and the jet-black filly didn't look particularly bothered. After all, she had been inside their stall nearly every day since the filly was born in April. Today didn't appear any different to the horses. She took a deep breath and exhaled to steady herself. Out of Nick's earshot, she whispered to Shenanigans, "Say goodbye, mama. Time for baby to grow up." She gave Shenanigans a pat as the mare nuzzled her baby. "Baby," Meg said, "you say goodbye, too. You gotta go learn how to race." She felt her lips trembling again.

"OPEN 'EM UP!" Nick called through the barn. On cue, Tuck slid his stall door open. Meg slid hers. They each led a baby out, and quickly turned to shut the stall doors before the mamas could follow them.

Just out of the stall, Ruffian planted her hind legs and squealed. She refused to leave her mama. As Meg tugged on the lead rope, Ruffian squealed louder. "Come on, girl, come on," she pleaded with the baby. "You've got a big job to do. You're gonna be a great racehorse just like your grand-daddy," Meg purred to the baby even though she had broken out in a hot sweat. Ruffian twitched her ears forward as if very interested in what Meg had just told her. The filly took a step forward with her right foot then her left and skipped out behind Meg. Relieved, Meg wiped her brow and gathered her courage.

Ruffian danced behind Meg as she led her out to the van and loaded her up. Tuck followed with another baby who was kicking and squealing all the way to the van. Tuck was sweat-soaked, too.

"Need a hand?" she asked.

"Worst. Day. Of. My. Life," Tuck grunted.

"You think you have it rough? Think of these babies," she said. "Here, let me try." She lowered her voice to a gentle whisper. "Come on, sweetheart. Be a good baby. It's time to go for a car ride. No big deal." Meg clucked to the baby and slowly led him onto the van.

They'd be moved to Raceland. It wasn't far, just five miles away. But for them, it would feel like a million miles away from their mothers.

CHAPTER 8

Promotion

Meg and Tuck rode along with Nick to Raceland. He wanted familiar hands to help the youngsters adjust to life in their new barn—without their mamas. Meg couldn't believe she was offered the chance to go to Raceland. It was like going to Wrigley Field for baseball fans. All the greats passed through these gates.

After unloading the horses to one of Raceland's rolling pastures, Tuck and Meg had lunch under a pine tree. Tuck, unwrapping the paper from his tuna sandwich, said, "It was a hard day. I've never seen anything so sad."

Meg, chewing her peanut butter sandwich, slugged Tuck on his upper arm. "Yeah, well, at least Nick didn't catch you blubbering away."

"What? You kidding me?"

"You heard me. I was getting all emotional thinking about them leaving their mamas. Nick walks up, sees me, and scolds me for it."

"I don't believe it."

She looked at Tuck out of the corner of her eye. "Believe it."

"I had no idea you would cry."

"Very funny, smart aleck." She didn't want people, even Tuck, thinking she couldn't handle things or wasn't tough enough to be in this business. They'd tell her to go home and join a Brownie troop or something.

"Seriously, Meg. I had no clue."

"Well, keep it between us, all right." She swallowed the last bite of her sandwich. "Nick was probably regretting hiring an *emotional female*."

"Hey! Kids! Move it," Nick hollered at them from across the pasture.

"Speak of the devil," Meg muttered to Tuck.

Nick strode toward them, his cowboy boots kicking up mud as he approached.

"Lunch break is over. You two need to get their stalls ready. Load 'em down with pine shavings and alfalfa. Rinse and fill two water buckets in each stall." Nick wiped the sweat off his brow with a handkerchief. "You'll find the wheelbarrows on the backside of the barn."

Within the hour, they set up two new stalls for their horses. The stalls, Meg thought, were crisp and clean. Cozy.

By four o'clock, Nick wanted all of the weanlings, as they were now officially called, brought into the new barn to have their supper and get settled in for the night.

Tuck and Meg went back to the weanling pasture. When the fillies and colts saw the kids, familiar faces from their old home, they nickered and romped toward them, eager for reassurance.

Meg clipped Ruffian's lead rope to her halter. Ruffian twitched her tail playfully. "How'd you do today, big girl?" She smiled up at the filly. Ruffian pawed at the dirt and blew out a wad of snot. "I guess it was a silly question. You can handle yourself just about anywhere. I shouldn't have worried about you at all."

Tuck's colt balked a bit on his lead rope but when Meg stepped in front of them with Ruffian on the lead, the colt quit his belly-aching and followed the girls quietly into the barn.

Ruffian, always ready for a meal, happily munched on her grain and alfalfa. Meg looked on. "You're going to do all right. You are a big, smart girl," she told the filly.

"You always talk to them like children?" a gruff voice came from behind Meg.

Meg felt herself blush three shades of crimson. Why was everyone catching her unawares today?

"Young lady? You going to be rude and not answer me?"

She turned around and met the eyes of a gray haired man. He had a serious face with deep-set eyes. He looked old enough to be her grandpa. He wore a fedora and thick, black rimmed eyeglasses. Even though his voice sounded gruff, Meg thought she saw a sparkle of delight ignite in his eyes.

"No, sir. I mean no disrespect, sir."

"Good. Now answer my question." This old man had a razor-sharp stare.

"What question?"

The man folded his arms across his chest and tucked his hands deep into his armpits. "Do you always talk to them like children?"

Meg glimpsed Tuck out of the corner of her eye. Tuck's face looked as pale as a daisy. He was terrified of this man, too, it seemed.

Straightening her shoulders, she replied, "I don't talk to them like children. I talk to them with respect. Sir." She was tired of people criticizing her—first Nick and now this fella.

"Why talk to 'em at all?" he asked.

"I find that talking to them makes them calmer, more relaxed, as they get to know people. It helps them so they can focus on being good horses in kindergarten. I, er, mean in training, sir."

The man tipped his hat back off his forehead. "How old are you, girl?"

"Fifteen, sir."

"Come back in a month. I've got a job for you."

He nodded at Meg and he strolled out of the barn. She exhaled after he left. *Good riddance,* she thought.

"Who was that guy?" she asked Tuck.

"You don't know? Are you kidding me? That was Frank Whiteley."

She shrugged. "So?"

"The famous horse trainer. The guy who trained Tom Rolfe and Damascus. Remember those names?"

Tuck and Doc had been teaching her about Thoroughbred bloodlines and racing history over the past six months. Meg jogged her memory. Tom Rolfe...Tom Rolfe had won the Preakness a few years back. And Damascus. Damascus carried the Preakness and the Belmont Stakes a few years after that.

Tuck interrupted Meg's thoughts, "He's only one of the most respected horse trainers in the business. And he just offered you a job."

"Holy cow!" Racing royalty, she realized.

Tuck laughed, "Holy cow is right. You just got yourself one heck of a promotion. Congratulations!"

Seated around the dinner table later that night, Meg fretted over how to break the news to her parents. The news that she would be working for a real horse trainer and not just Uncle Doc anymore. Mom had put up a fight when Doc had hired her on to help with the foals. But Aunt Louise had worked her magic and convinced Mom that working for Doc would keep Meg busy so she wouldn't hole herself up in her room all of the time. It wasn't the ideal situation, at least from Mom's perspective, but if it got a sullen girl out of the house, as Louise pointed out, Mom had nothing to complain about.

Meg didn't expect Mom to cave in so easily this time. Chumming around with Uncle Doc was one thing. Working, really working, for a racehorse trainer, was another matter altogether. This job seemed less like family time and more like business. Meg knew her mother would fuss because a job with Frank at Raceland would take her even deeper into the horse business. It didn't sound much like a simple distraction or hobby for a girl. It was a job. Maybe even a career.

Dad was always working at the bank, providing for them. He didn't pay much mind to the comings and goings of his family, truth be told. Mom, however, wanted her to become a lady and stop hanging around horse people all the time. She'd told Meg she'd never find a good husband at a barn. Then Mom would huff and puff her chest out, signaling an end to the conversation. Mom didn't realize that being with the horses was all Meg cared about. It wasn't about hanging around cowboys or catching a husband. It was about those big, complicated, wonderful horses.

Even though Meg knew the storm that was to come, she decided to break the news to her parents real quick. No sweet talking. "Mom, Frank Whiteley offered me a real job today."

Mom laid her fork down, smoothed the cloth napkin over her lap. "Pardon me? Who?"

"Frank Whiteley. The racehorse trainer." Meg lowered her voice, hoping to show her mother some respect and not ruffle her feathers.

Dad looked up from his mashed potatoes and gravy.

"Every day after school. And on weekends."

Mom answered, "Absolutely not. You've got school work to do. You work enough already with Doc. Furthermore, you are a sophomore now." She paused, then lowered her voice, "You need friends your own age. Not old horsemen. No man wants a ding-bat for a wife, or a rough neck." She pushed her shoulders back. "Besides, all that sun will ruin your complexion."

Meg felt the electric tension in the air between them. *Jeezus,* she thought, *is it 1950 or 1972?* When had Mom turned into such a WASP? There had been a time when Mom would run barefoot down by the river, and splash in its snow-fed waters with all of the other young mothers and children. *Where'd you go, Mom,* she wanted to ask, *where'd you go?*

Dad attempted to calm the stormy situation. "Meg's only a kid, sweetheart. She's got plenty of time to worry about catching a husband."

"Look at her, she looks like a boy. Dressing in blue jeans and cotton t-shirts. Dirty boots. She looks like a ruffian."

Meg stifled a giggle. *Ruffian,* she thought. *There's no one else*

I'd rather be if I could.

"Suzanne. Really, sweetheart. She will be fine. Doc works with this Frank character, too. Doc'll be around plenty to check on her. To make sure she isn't turning into one of those fool hardy jocks. Plus, it will give you extra time to join the ladies at the club for Bridge. Build those influential friendships for us, my dear." Fortune smiled on Meg. Dad was too tired for an argument. He wanted to smooth over the tension and have a quiet supper.

"Your brother is a bad influence on my daughter," Mom spat as her eyes darted from Meg to Dad. Although she thought Mom might be softening a bit at the suggestion of more country club time with the ladies.

"Meg, honey, how are you going to get back and forth?" Dad asked.

"I can hitch a ride with Doc or Aunt Louise. Don't worry about it. We've got it all figured out."

"If your grades slip, that's the end of it. You hear?"

"Yes, sir!" Meg jumped up from her seat. She ran to her father and wrapped her arms around his neck. "Thank you."

He patted her back. "Go on, finish your supper."

CHAPTER 9

Yearling Training

November 1972

J ust as requested by Frank Whiteley, Meg returned to Raceland a month later. Nick sauntered up to Meg, greeting her, this time, with a devilishly wide smile on his face.

"Meg Murphy, congratulations. Getting hired by Mr. Whiteley himself!" Nick shook Meg's hand, pumping it hard.

"Thank you, Nick. I'm honored to be hired by him."

"Frank is in South Carolina now, working the two-year-olds in Camden. You're going to work with me, as a groom, with these here yearlings. We'll get 'em ready to ship to Frank." Nick, leading Meg into the office said, "You'll help me teach them how to take a bit, a saddle, and how to hold a rider. It's tough work. Often dangerous. You'll likely get kicked, nipped, or bucked. Think you can handle it?" Nick's eyes narrowed. He was trying to intimidate her. To scare her off.

"Yes, sir," she said without a hint of worry in her voice.

"All right. Finish this paperwork. Then we've got work to do."

After she finished the new hire paperwork, they walked over to Ruffian's stall.

"There's your first one of the day. You'll work her for a time.

When she gets tired, you can move on to the next one. Don't work the young ones too much. Their little brains can only handle so much at a time. Have patience with them."

"Yes, sir, always," Meg answered.

"Holler if you need anything."

Nick walked away, leaving her alone with Ruffian.

"Hey, girl, remember me? How are you?" She stepped into the stall.

Ruffian did a shuffle with her front hooves. She lifted her nose in the air. As if recognizing Meg's scent, she lowered her head toward Meg.

Scratching the star on Ruffian's forehead, Meg whispered, "Oh silly girl, I've missed you." She had never been around a horse like Ruffian before, a horse who could look deep into your eyes and who just seemed to get you. Then she remembered Buckwheat. He'd been like that, too.

She reached into her pocket and slipped Ruffian a molasses cookie. "A treat for a growing girl." She stroked Ruffian's neck.

Ruffian gummed the chewy treat, her long tongue flopping out of her mouth, savoring the gooey cookie.

As Meg gave Ruffian her first lesson, she talked to her to keep her calm. "They call it breaking but we're not breaking anything," Meg reassured Ruffian. "We are teaching you." Ruffian flicked her ears forward. Meg knew how independent this filly was. She planned to take it nice and easy with her. No surprises. And, most importantly, she wanted to let this filly think that she was in control. No harshness. Lots of rewards. Meg placed the saddle pad softly on Ruffian's back. Ruffian grumbled and balked.

Meg cooed to her, calming the filly. When Ruffian settled down, she lifted the saddle pad off her back. "Good girl. I think that's enough for today."

The next afternoon, Meg entered Ruffian's stall with a shiny piece of silver. Ruffian scooted backwards, away from the foreign object.

"Aww, girl, look here. This is a bit. It goes in your mouth like so." She held the silver bit up to her own mouth, opened wide, and slid it over her tongue. She choked back a gag and took the bit out of her mouth.

Ruffian nickered and shook her head like she was trying to say "no."

Meg did it again, placing the bit close to her own mouth.

Ruffian took a step closer, inspecting this strange object and this even stranger human. Ruffian ran her nose across the bit, taking in the smell of Meg's minty toothpaste that was now all over the bit.

"Here, girl. Let's try it on." She took Ruffian's nose in her hands, and tried to slide the bit between Ruffian's lips. Ruffian reared.

Letting out a sigh, Meg pulled out a molasses cookie from her jacket pocket. She wiped the cookie all over the bit. "Yuummm, yum," she whispered to Ruffian.

Never one to refuse food, Ruffian became curious. She crept closer to Meg and the scary silver object. Her nose twitched faster. Molasses. Ruffian gummed the bit.

"Attagirl." Meg saw her opportunity. She gently but firmly took Ruffian's mouth in her hands, and slid the bit into the horse's mouth. Before Ruffian could balk, Meg cooed to her, "What a good girl you are. What a big, smart girl." She petted Ruffian's cheek, held the bit in for a minute longer as the filly started to snort and pull away. "See, it's not so bad, is it?" Meg released the bit from Ruffian's mouth, gave her another pat, and this time, held a molasses cookie out to Ruffian as a reward.

Ruffian snuffled about and then decided it would be best to eat the cookie.

Meg placed the bit outside of the stall, so Ruffian couldn't see it. She didn't want to stress out the young horse. "I am so proud of you. Day Two in school and you've already had a bit in your mouth. Good girl!" Meg patted her and then groomed her to calm her down.

Nick walked up as Meg was praising Ruffian. "Frank warned me that you're a talker."

Meg, puzzled by this remark, didn't answer.

Nick added, "I like grooms who talk to their horses. Treat 'em with respect, like they are thinking creatures. I like it. Keep it up, gal."

She smiled, surprised at Nick's approval. *Maybe he wasn't so bad after all?* She was glad to be fitting in at the new barn.

Breaking horses was new territory for Meg. She'd ridden for a few years, most of the time on old Quarter Horses, sound old campaigners, trail horses. Breaking young horses was riskier and required patience. Most of the time, she likened herself to a school teacher, giving practice exercises to her young students, and praising them profusely when they finally got it right. For some of the yearlings, that meant Meg had to do the same thing over and over again a hundred times before they finally got it. Plenty of treats and pats when they mastered their equine ABCs.

Ruffian, on the other hand, learned most things fairly quick. She learned to take the bit in just a couple of days. Then Meg attached the bit to the bridle. After a day of taking the bridle on and off a half dozen times, Ruffian wore it like a pro.

When Nick gave Meg the red saddle cloth and girth strap to lay over Ruffian's back, the horse looked wild-eyed. But, with Meg's soft words, Ruffian settled down, and let Meg place the saddle cloth and girth over her back without a problem.

"You are a champion," Meg told Ruffian. She leaned closer to the filly. "You are the smartest creature in this barn, too." Ruffian whinnied in pleasure.

Two weeks later, Nick brought the racing saddle out.

"Here's the real test. Think she's ready for it?" He asked both Meg and the horse.

"As ready as she'll ever be," Meg replied.

"Hold her bridle," Nick said. Then he quietly slid the saddle over Ruffian's back. Her breathing increased. "Watch yourself, in case she goes to rear," Nick added. "She could kill you."

"Got her."

Ruffian started to sweat on her withers. But she didn't rear.

"Good girl," Meg smiled at Ruffian. When the horse read Meg's body language, her breathing slowed down to normal.

"There, there, it's nothing but a little bitty saddle, just like the big racehorses wear."

Nick raised an eyebrow at Meg.

Meg said, "Sometimes she just needs to hear the reason

behind things."

Nick let the saddle rest on Ruffian's back for a few more minutes.

"Tomorrow, I want you to do this. If she takes it well, you're to slide your body across her back."

Meg, confused, wrinkled her brow.

"With your belly. Flop yourself over her back, on your belly. She needs to get used to weight on her back."

"Like a circus rider?"

"Something like that. And wear a helmet."

The next morning, Meg placed the saddlecloth over Ruffian. The horse barely flinched. Meg put the racing saddle across Ruffian's back. She reached under Ruffian's belly to cinch the girth, and that's when Ruffian turned, folded her ears back, bared her teeth, squealed, and nipped at Meg's arm. A banshee.

She jumped back from Ruffian. "Hey!" She yelled. "What was that for?"

Ruffian looked Meg right in the eyes. She was ready to bite again.

"That wasn't nice manners, young lady," she scolded Ruffian. "I'll have to tie you up." Meg clipped Ruffian's bridle to the hook on the wall, just tight enough so that Ruffian couldn't bend her neck around and take a chunk out of her arm. Ruffian snorted again at her predicament. She didn't like confinement.

Meg reached under her belly, tightened the girth. Ruffian grunted a few times but gave up the fight. "I know that girth is probably tight around your fat baby belly, but you'll get used to how it feels. Just like wearing a belt." She lifted up her t-shirt to show Ruffian her belted blue jeans. Ruffian stamped her front hoof in frustration.

"Now, now, settle down. I'm going to climb up here and sit on you for a short while." Ruffian's attitude made Meg feel skittish. She checked the chinstrap on her helmet before she got near the horse again. Secured.

Ruffian's eyes grew big. Meg swung herself over Ruffian's back. Belly down, just as Nick had said. The horse squealed and flailed, trying to buck her off.

"Whoa, girl, whoa." Meg slid gingerly to the ground, feet first. She rubbed Ruffian's side to soothe her. She noticed Ruffian was sweating, clearly panicking with the new lesson.

"You did great, girl," she said. "We'll try this again tomorrow." Meg was only half-lying as she slowly unsaddled Ruffian. She didn't want to frighten the young horse. One bad training session could instantly undo all their hard work. This horse had a sound brain and Meg didn't want to upset her.

Ruffian's muscles relaxed when the saddle came off. She gave her great, black body a shake, like a dog shaking off water after a bath. "See, you survived. You'll be okay," Meg said as she left the stall. She had five other yearlings to repeat this exercise with today. She didn't have too much time to waste playing. Besides, Mom was getting annoyed with all the time Meg spent at the barn and wanted her home before seven o'clock. Mom wanted her to join the cheerleading squad and do normal teenage stuff. Safe stuff. But strutting around in a short skirt, shaking her tail at boys, didn't sound like much fun to Meg. She'd rather work with the horses, especially this beautiful creature. She was something special. Ruffian was regal. She didn't take no guff from anyone.

She didn't need to fit in with any crowd. Teenagers, on the other hand, were so petty and insecure. *Why couldn't Mom understand that?*

The next day went smoother than the one before. Meg managed to slide across Ruffian. The horse didn't spook or snap at her. She stood quietly while Meg stretched across her back. Meg was on her belly having a deep philosophical conversation about boys with the horse.

"All they care about is looks. Seriously. I'm sick of it. Why can't they just grow up? When are they gonna realize that there's more to a girl than how pretty she is? Or how big her boobs are. What about brains? Smarts? Or a sense of humor?" Meg took a breath.

Ruffian twitched her ears, listening to Meg's tirade about boys. "My mom says to give these boys a chance. Someday, she says, I'll want to find a nice boy and settle down and have babies. *Good grief.* As if I'm a broodmare or something. No offense to your mother," Meg patted Ruffian's belly. She could feel the blood rushing to her head as she hung upside down from the horse. Ruffian was actually taking this session very well. "You horses. Now that's what I admire. You don't take crap from anyone. And you can tell a big, fat fake as soon as you see one. No one is going to fool you or take advantage of you. No way. You know why? Because you have confidence. You have confidence in yourself. In your strength. In your smarts. You don't need no boy telling you what you're worth. Huh?"

Ruffian shifted her weight on her back legs. Meg, staring at the stall floor, lifted her head when Ruffian moved. Nick. He was standing outside the stall, listening to Meg's dramatic monologue.

"Good grief," Meg mumbled as she slid off Ruffian. "Men."

"How is your horse therapy going today?" Nick asked her. He appeared to be fighting back a smirk. How much of her rant did he hear? So hilarious. She decided to pretend it didn't happen. She would try to act perfectly natural, not like some silly teenager. She was a groom after all.

"Ruffian is great. Taking to my weight like it's a walk in the park." Meg dusted the dirt off her shirt and blue jeans.

"I see that. Another few sessions and then you're going to actually sit in the saddle."

She could tell Nick was proud of their progress despite her personal confessions to the horse.

By the end of the week, Meg was sitting upright on Ruffian. She had stirrups attached to the saddle, too. "Look at you. All grown up," she scratched Ruffian's neck. Ruffian nickered. It was as if the horse understood all that she said.

Ruffian wasn't quite ready to have a rider on her back for long periods of time. She was still a tad skittish with the saddle. Besides, her young bones were still developing and shouldn't be carrying all of Meg's 130 pounds just yet. Their lessons under saddle would be short, but daily.

This afternoon, Meg pressed her leg against Ruffian's belly, asking her to turn to the left. Ruffian curved her body, turning a clean figure eight in the pen. Meg changed legs and asked her, with the pressure of her legs, to go the opposite way. Ruffian responded and bent her body around and around again, enjoying the challenge, the mental stimulation.

After a dozen figure eights, Meg relaxed her leg pressure and slackened the reins. She leaned forward to stroke Ruffian's neck. "Well done. If you don't turn into a racehorse, we might make you into a cutting horse," she joked with Ruffian, trying to imagine this sleek creature working cows out west. *As if.* Ruffian didn't like the joke. She tucked her head down and bucked. Meg, caught off guard, flew through the air and landed in the dirt.

"Rapscallion," she scolded the horse as she got up and brushed herself off.

Ruffian, as still as a statue, gave Meg a droll, unfazed look.

"You rascal." Meg got back on the horse. "Let's do a few more figure eights. We can't end class with me in the dirt."

This time Meg didn't let her guard down. She had forgotten that Ruffian was still green and mischievous. But she wouldn't again.

Two more weeks went by, and Meg and Donnie Bussell, another groom, were taking turns riding Ruffian each day. Meg would handle the lighter work days, the days when Nick wanted Ruffian to walk and trot around the arena. Donnie, the more experienced rider, handled the heavier work days, the days when Nick wanted to see Ruffian canter and change leads from left to right or right to left. Often, on the days Meg wasn't riding, she'd hang out on the fence rail and watch Donnie work the filly and breeze her down the training track. She didn't understand how men as small and light as birds could work such thundering horses.

"How's she doing today?" Meg called across the track to Donnie.

"Nice and easy," Donnie paused as he prodded his left calf into Ruffian's side, asking her to canter. Ruffian felt his cue and

70

transitioned cleanly into the next gait. "She moves like a cat, so quiet."

When he came near Meg again, she said, "Squeaky and some of the grooms are taking to calling her Sofie."

"Why is that?" He clucked his tongue and signaled for Ruffian to pick up her pace.

"Cause she's so soft and smooth. Just like a sofa."

Donnie laughed. After a few strides, he brought Ruffian down to a trot, then a walk. He gave her a pat on her side. "Don't you have homework to do? What does your mama think about you hanging out at the barn on your days off?" He tried to sound all serious but Meg knew he was fooling around.

"I've got some English homework but I'd rather be here bothering you."

Donnie hopped off Ruffian. The horse bent down and rubbed her forehead up and down his side. "Hey, personal space, please," he said as he pushed the large filly out of his face.

Meg took the reins from him. "I'll take her back to the barn and hose her down."

"Thanks, kid. You're all right." He slapped Meg on her back like a big brother would. "But I wasn't joking about school work. You gotta study and do good. You don't want to be mucking stalls all your life, breaking your back, do you?"

Meg shrugged. "I don't know. I just know I want to be around horses and nothing else."

"I get it, kid. Trust me, I get it."

The water splashed over Ruffian's face, withers, and then her hind quarters. Meg loved bathing the horses. She loved scrubbing the sweat and grime off of them. She loved how their coats glistened as the water rained down on them. How they pinned their ears back as the water splashed their faces. How they lapped at the water with their velvet tongues, trying to drink from the fresh, cool spray.

As Meg lathered the shampoo across Ruffian's dark coat, the filly rumbled in contentment. She rinsed Ruffian and watched the soap suds run down the filly's long legs and swirl around the drain in the wash rack. When Meg was satisfied that the shampoo was rinsed clean, she took the sweat scraper and with large, swift downward strokes, flicked the excess water off of Ruffian's coat. She ran a dry towel across Ruffian's face. "Peek-a-boo, I see you," she laughed to the horse. Ruffian shook her head away from the towel, not wanting to play.

"You must be hungry. Is that why you don't want to play?"

Ruffian pawed the wash rack floor. She raised her tail and left Meg a large, steaming present.

"Gee, thanks," Meg said to Ruffian as she went to get the shovel and wheelbarrow to haul away the manure.

She finished toweling Ruffian's legs, rubbing them firmly to squeeze off the excess water. Then she stepped back to admire Ruffian. The horse looked like an ancient Roman statue, sculpted sleek and smooth.

"You are gorgeous."

Ruffian batted her large brown eyes at Meg.

"And don't you know it." Meg didn't even try to hide her amusement. She felt like the luckiest girl alive—to work with such a horse.

CHAPTER 10

The Training Track

November 12, 1973

John Sosby, one of Frank's trainers, led Ruffian to the one-mile training track. Nick, perched on the horse's back, adjusted his helmet. Nick wouldn't dare let Meg climb aboard Ruffian for her first real timed run on the track because he said you never knew what to expect. The training track was Nick's area of expertise. He'd ridden these young ones for years. Even though Meg pleaded with Nick to let her ride, he wouldn't budge. "I don't want no kid getting killed on my watch." As a consolation, he said, "But you can be the official training timer." They needed to record Ruffian's training times to see her potential.

"What do you think she's got?" Nick asked them.

"Hard to tell," John said as he unclipped the lead rope from Ruffian's bridle. "Let's just see if you can get her to run. Ready?"

Nick positioned Ruffian so she'd go counter clockwise around the track. They'd only run a half mile today.

At the rail, John yelled, "Ready. Set. Go!"

Meg hit the start button on the timer.

Ruffian froze.

"Come on, girl," Nick urged her. "Come on, run!" He kicked Ruffian in her sides to get her to move and Ruffian shot forward like a greyhound in hot pursuit of its quarry.

And, boy howdy, did she run.

"Slow her!" John yelled.

Ruffian galloped around the far turn. Effortless. Her tail floating in the wind.

Meg could see Nick yanking at the reins, trying to pull her up. Ruffian felt the tugging at the bit in her mouth. She danced left to right. Nick, still pulling, called out "whoa, whoa, whoa."

Ruffian, wild-eyed, slowed down to a canter, then a trot. By the time they reached Meg and John, Ruffian was at the walk. Nick was in a frothy sweat.

"Why the heck did you run her like that? Her bones are too soft for hard work." John was beyond angry with Nick. Meg knew he didn't take any chances with the Thoroughbreds in his care. "I told you nice and easy so she could get a feel for the track."

Nick slid off Ruffian's back. He unclipped his helmet, throwing it at John's feet. "Do you think I wanted her to go like that? A freaking thunder bolt of lightning. I could barely hang on."

To diffuse the situation, Meg stepped between the two men. "I know," Meg interjected quietly, hoping to soothe their tempers and not upset Ruffian. "You wouldn't push her too hard." Meg noticed that Ruffian's eyes looked eager. The horse hadn't even broken a sweat. She looked like she was ready to run some more. To her equine brain, Nick had only given her a short warm up. She was anxiously awaiting the next go 'round.

John shoved his hands into his jacket pockets. "Meg," he snapped, "Take her to the wash racks and cool her down."

Meg walked Ruffian to the barn. There, she bathed her, splashing extra water on the filly's face. Ruffian smacked her lips out and swiped her tongue across the stream of cool water that shot from the hose. "Those fellas haven't seen nothing yet. Have they? You were just getting warmed up when Nick stopped you." She shut the hose off. "You are going to be a fine racehorse. I bet you'll be the fastest filly in the world."

Ruffian whinnied. She agreed.

Nick came back through the barn, leading a giant red horse. The red horse looked like it was dancing a jig on the lead rope. Jaunty. Confident. Enormous. Almost as big as Ruffian. Seeing the larger-than-life stallion, Ruffian raised her nose in the air and sang out to him. "Shush!" Meg said. "Don't make a fool of yourself for a boy...horse."

"Take a look here!" Nick called out to her.

She set her towel down and walked closer to the red monster.

"Who is this one?"

"You don't recognize him?"

Meg shook her head.

"Not at all? Not even one little iota?"

"Nope."

"This is Secretariat. Ring a bell?"

"Omygoshohmygosh," she exclaimed. She was standing right in front of the world famous Triple Crown winner. Secretariat won the Kentucky Derby, the Preakness, and the Belmont Stakes. Fans called him "Big Red" because of his size and speed. He wasn't just any old boy horse. He was the best Thoroughbred of them all.

Nick, delighted that reality finally hit Meg, added, "Go ahead. Pet him."

Meg reached out and tenderly stroked Secretariat's deep red coat. He nudged her side with his nose. She laughed. "I think he's looking for a cookie."

Nick gave the lead rope a firm, quick tug to signal to Secretariat to stop nosing around.

"Why is he here?" she asked.

"He's heading to Claiborne to stud. Any of his offspring will sell for thousands of dollars after his big wins."

Meg heard the rumblings of car engines outside the barn.

Nick sighed. "Agh. The press. As soon as word got out that Secretariat was coming to Kentucky, we've been getting phone calls all morning. Reporters want interviews and photographs. John told me to move Big Red real fast."

Meg, stunned, could only utter, "WOW." Secretariat. The Press. This here was the big time.

"Yeah, right. I wish they'd leave us alone. We've got plenty of work to do around here. Last thing I want to do is waste time talking to newspaper people. I've still got five more horses to exercise today."

Nick gave the lead rope a short snap and led Secretariat to the far end of the barn, out the back doors to the far paddock. Meg realized he was leading Secretariat as far away from the reporters as he possibly could.

Three days later, Meg got orders to prepare Ruffian for a

move. She was headed out of state for training. She needed to go to Frank in South Carolina. Nick gave her a list of all of Ruffian's gear to pack on the horse trailer, including food and vitamin supplements.

"Check them off as you load them. Don't forget a single one," Nick instructed.

"Yes, sir."

"With all the excitement about Secretariat here, maybe we can sneak this one out," Nick said almost under his breath. "Listen, kid, don't tell any reporters where she's going or what's her name."

"Sure."

"No. No *sures*. Do not say a word. And DO NOT tell them how fast she is. Got it?"

"Yes, sir." Meg lifted her chin, confidently, as if signaling to Nick that she was all business. She could handle it. *No problemo.*

"We can't have any of our training secrets leaked to our competition. This filly is something special but nobody but us can know that. At least not yet."

Meg realized why Nick was so adamant about keeping Ruffian's identity a secret. This horse had promise. Potential. She could be a real star someday. Meg smiled at Nick, "I'll get 'Sofie' all taken care of. Don't worry about it, boss."

Nick winked at her. "Thanks, Meg. Get Sofie all taken care of. I can always distract those reporters with Secretariat while you load her up." Meg was smart and she knew Nick appreciated the fact that she'd use Ruffian's barn nickname to hide her from the prying press.

As Nick walked away, Meg realized Ruffian was leaving her. Off to complete her training and then who knew? If she survived and did well, she'd be off to the tracks all over the country. The odds were Meg would never see her beautiful, playful filly again.

CHAPTER 11

South Carolina Bound

November 16, 1973

Autumn was settling over the countryside. Frost covered the bluegrass. Leaves turned copper. Now, before morning turnouts in the pastures, the grooms covered their horses in crimson blankets to keep them warm. The horses, who trained on the racetrack early in the morning, were especially frisky as the cold air tickled their nostrils and gave their strides an extra bounce.

Ruffian had done well training under Nick, learning how to be handled under saddle and on the lead rope. She didn't fuss much—only when she wanted her dinner. Meg, proud of the filly, hated to see her go. But Nick said it was time, so it was time. Meg also knew that Nick wanted to keep Ruffian out of the eyes of the press, so no one would leak the news of her speed to their competition. And, with Secretariat around, the press was never far enough away. She had to go to South Carolina to train with Frank. Mr. and Mrs. Janney arranged it as fast as they could. Frank would get Ruffian ready to officially race as a two-year-old. After meeting Frank Whiteley, Meg knew Ruffian would be fine. He was one of the best in the business. He was said to be tough, strict, yet careful. Meg, though, would miss Ruffian and their girl talks as they exercised. Part of her wished Ruffian could just stay in Kentucky and be a pet. That thought made her laugh, imagining Ruffian lounging around in a suburban backyard, getting fat and sassy. Ruffian would go stir crazy with no place to run. As if Ruffian could ever settle down and not run! She was cut from a different cloth. Meg could see it plain as day—ever since Ruffian was a little thing, flying across the pasture with the other foals. She'd barrel past the foals, kicking, rearing, and singing out in satisfaction. God, was she magnificent.

A truck's horn broke Meg's reverie. The horse trailer was waiting to haul Ruffian to South Carolina. The driver, getting impatient, pounded on the horn again.

"Can he chill out?" Meg snipped to Ruffian.

Most of the trailer had been loaded. Meg had packed Ruffian's water, hay, and grain supply, as well as her blankets. The last thing to do was load the horse.

She choked back tears as she walked Ruffian up to the horse trailer.

Ruffian nuzzled her large, black nose into Meg's neck. Meg stroked her face and whispered to the horse, "You be a good girl. You hear? Show those colts on the track what you got though."

Meg wiped her nose on her shirt sleeve. She had taken care of Ruffian since she was born. Meg patted Ruffian's neck. "I'll look for you in the newspapers. I bet you'll be a champion."

Tuck jogged toward them. "Come on, the driver wants to hit the road. Get her on the trailer."

"I am. Just wanted to say goodbye." Meg said, and stopped, stunned at seeing Tuck. "What are you doing here?" She hadn't seen Tuck in ages, since they loaded the weanlings at Claiborne. At school, he'd been busy with football practice and flirting with the girls. He didn't pay her any mind. Odd, she thought, after how friendly they had become. It was as if he didn't want anyone to know that he did manual labor or something. "Don't I get a nice *hello, how are you doing?*"

"Sorry!" Tuck groaned.

"Miss me? We don't work together anymore. You don't even bother to talk to me at school."

Tuck hung his head, "Yeah, well, we move in different circles at school. Your science friends kinda intimidate me."

Meg cracked a smile. Intimidated by her friends? A slight inferiority complex. Who would have guessed?

Tuck grinned back at Meg. "You betcha I miss working with you. Things are quiet around Claiborne without you," he kidded. Tuck leaned closer to Meg so no one could overhear them. "How'd you like working with Nick over here?" Gossip around the barn was never tolerated, especially if it was the hired help doing the gossiping.

"It's good," she answered. "Keeps me hopping. He's strict. To the tee about everything. Big job to do, you know?"

"Yeah, if Nick doesn't get 'em ready right, Frank will have his hide," Tuck said. He added, "I might be getting a promotion, too."

"No way."

"Mr. Whiteley asked Doc to go along when they haul Ruffian to South Carolina. Make sure she is safe and sound. Doc asked me to give him a hand so I get to go along for the ride." Tuck looked excited about his road trip, but he paused, noticing Meg's

81

red rimmed eyes. "You been crying?"

"No. Don't be stupid."

"You were. You were crying like a baby over this horse."

"So what?"

"So what? She's not yours, you know."

"I know."

Tuck lowered his eyes. "Hey, I'm sorry, Meg." Tuck looked embarrassed for trying to pick on Meg. His teasing had landed all wrong.

The driver honked the truck's horn again. Doc hopped out of the passenger's side of the cab and shouted, "Come on, kids. Get her on board."

"Yes, sir," Meg called out.

They loaded Ruffian onto the trailer. Meg patted Ruffian's side. "Be safe, sweet girl."

Tuck shut the trailer door and locked it.

"Why do you kids look like you're heading to a funeral?" Doc asked, climbing back into the truck.

Protectively, Tuck spoke up, "I guess it's hard to say goodbye."

Doc looked from Tuck to Meg. "It does tug at your heart. But it's not goodbye forever. It's so long for now."

"Yes, sir," Meg sniffled. Why were goodbyes so hard for her? Especially with this horse.

"Hey, kids, come on." Doc said as he tried to cheer them up. "What do you say we make plans to go see Ruffian in her first race?"

At the prospect of seeing Ruffian again, Meg perked up.

"Next year?"

"Yep. Your parents will let you take a road trip to a stakes race for sure." Doc gave Meg a wink for reassurance. "I'll talk them into it. I promise."

"That's a plan, Doc," Tuck said matter-of-factly. "Don't you forget about it neither."

"I never go back on my promises, son. All a man's got is his word."

Doc slid across the bench seat. Tuck jumped in next to him, and motioned to the driver that it was all clear to go. Meg watched as the horse trailer rumbled down the tree- lined road, taking Ruffian away to start her new life, far away from the Kentucky bluegrass. Far away from home. Meg trudged back to the barn to finish her chores.

CHAPTER 12

Attitude Adjustment

January 1974

With fewer young horses, since most had either been sold off or shipped to South Carolina to train with Frank, Nick cut Meg's work hours. He didn't need all the extra hands around until the next crop of youngsters came in. Instead of hanging around the barn every day of the week, Meg was forced to focus on school and act like a "normal teenager" as her Mom said. She was halfway through junior year. The year that mattered most on college applications. She did well in her classes, especially biology. The way cells functioned interested her. Growing, changing, taking on new traits. Every other subject seemed kind of drab in comparison, like a bowl of steamed cauliflower that you're told to eat because it's good for you, but it's certainly nothing remarkable.

The worst part of the school day was not in her classes though. It was at lunch—the social time of the day. Meg still felt like nobody really wanted to hang out with her except for Sarah and Eliza. She wasn't in the band so she didn't sit with the band kids. She wasn't dating a football player so she couldn't sit with the jocks. She certainly was not happy about the war in Vietnam but she wasn't one of the anti-war protesters, "the beatnik hippies" according to her dad, so she didn't sit with those kids. It was just her, Eliza, and Sarah, seated in a corner in the cafeteria. They didn't seem to mind not being noticed, not having a large group of friends. But Meg did. She felt the loneliness tug at her heart more often than she cared to admit. And it only continued to remind her of what she had left behind in Montana. Here, kids still knocked into her in the hallways and didn't even bother to say "excuse me." She was that bowl of cauliflower. She remembered back home with her old friends, going fishing and riding together. Camping. Yet, here, the boys did certain things. Hunt, fish, be manly. And the girls did certain things. Dress up, smile pretty, flirt. Separate and not equal, from Meg's point of view. Here Meg was barely noticeable. Not gorgeous. Not ugly. Just nothing remarkable amongst her classmates.

With Ruffian gone and not much barn time to speak of, Meg got lonesome. She decided to try to make up with her mom. They hadn't always argued like wild cats, only after the move to Kentucky. Why was Mom always trying so hard to forget Montana and fit in the South? Heck, she even wore pearls to the supermarket.

After school, Meg trotted into the kitchen to find fresh biscuits cooling on the countertop. She tugged at the corner of a biscuit, tearing a small piece off, and popped it into her mouth. Mom came through the door, catching her.

"That's for supper!" she said. "If you want a snack, take an apple." Mom took a bright green apple from the glass bowl on the table and handed it to her. Meg rubbed it off on her shirt and took a large bite. She chomped and chomped on the tart apple.

"Really, Megan, you eat like a horse."

Meg chose to ignore that comment. She crunched on the apple loudly just to annoy her. Her resolution to be civilized to her mother forgotten for the moment.

"Cheerleading tryouts are today. Six o'clock at the gym. Why don't you go?"

Meg swallowed the apple hard. She saw her mother's eager expression.

"You used to love gymnastics and tumbling when you were little. Remember?"

That seemed like a gazillion years ago. Bouncing on trampolines and walking on balance beams in the makeshift gymnastics studio that had been in the old auto repair garage. She had loved the thrill of rolling and flying through the air. Most of all she had loved Mom cheering for her. How old had she been? Not more than five or six. Well before the move to Kentucky.

Making the cheerleading squad would instantly make Meg part of the popular crowd. She knew that's exactly what her mother hoped for—a twinkling, radiant, people-pleaser for a daughter. Instead, she had a loner who preferred horses to people. Luck of the draw, Meg thought ironically. "Sure, Mom, sure," Meg conceded. She'd go to tryouts if it would make Mom happy. But Meg had a plan. She wanted to see Mom happy so that she would agree to let her go to New York with Doc to see Ruffian race. It was a big, fabulous plan. Keep the parents happy, give them what they want and voila! They just wouldn't be able to refuse her teensy request to go watch a horse race in New York with her uncle. Could they?

Mom practically danced around the kitchen, "I'll comb your hair and show you how to put on a little makeup. You'll be terrific!" She squeezed Meg and squealed, "We can spend some quality time together. Finally!" Man, did Mom ever want a girlie-girl for a kid.

After allowing Mom to primp and prep her for nearly an hour, Mom dropped her off at the school gym at 5:45 so she could stretch and get warmed up before tryouts.

"Knock their socks off, sweetie," Mom said as she waved goodbye.

Meg walked through the double doors, her freckled face painted with rosy-red blush and sparkling pink lip gloss, her normally tousled hair slicked back in a perky ponytail and tied with a blue and silver ribbon—the school colors, of course. Forty-five girls gathered around the basketball court. Every single one of them wore short skirts, tight shirts, and had wide smiles with dazzling white teeth. Not a hair was out of place on any of them. They were all perky, peppy, freshly scrubbed and squeaky-clean. "Show ponies," Meg muttered under her breath. Was this nonsense worth it? Would trying out for the squad appease her mom? Would it guarantee that she could go see Ruffian race? Man, it better.

The girls bent and stretched, going through their warm-ups. Even though the girls looked as wholesome as Wonder Bread, Meg overheard a few of them laughing about getting to second base. They rolled their eyes at Meg, the newbie. She found a place to warm up at the far end of the gym.

A whistle-toting, hard-edged, sunburnt coach strode across the gymnasium. "Ladies, ladies, ladies! Line up!" Coach clapped loudly. The whistle shrieked. Girls jumped to the court perimeter. Coach walked down the line, examining each girl, stopping to write notes on her clipboard. Meg held back a giggle. *She's a little like Mrs. Janney with her horses except her horses are smarter than these girls,* Meg thought.

"You're soft, sweetie. Lay off the cookies if you want to make my squad," Coach said to a brunette next to Meg.

Coach strode up to Meg, eyeing her from head to toe, then circling around her, examining her backside. Meg felt like a piece of meat.

"Hmm, muscular build. Not too fat. Calves are a tad large for a girl. You might make a decent base for our pyramids." Coach tapped her pencil to the clipboard. She narrowed her eyes at Meg. "Play any other sports?"

"No, ma'am. Just horseback riding."

Coach recoiled. "Dance lessons? Gymnastics?"

Meg shook her head. "No, ma'am. Not since I was little. Just horse stuff now."

Coach wrinkled her nose and went to the next girl in line.

Over the next hour, the girls had to learn a cheer, kick their legs in the air in unison and shake their pom-poms. Coach blew the whistle. Time to build a pyramid out of their bodies. And smile. Big, bold, happy smiles. Meg was the base. Of course. Girls piled on her. She felt a lot like a pack mule.

Coach blew her whistle three times to signal the end of tryouts and waved the girls to the center of the court. Meg rubbed her sore back. She could feel every muscle and vertebrae in her back from the pyramid drill.

"The team list will be posted outside the girl's locker room by next Wednesday. If your name is on the list, I'll see you at practice on Thursday at 3:30. Goodnight, ladies. And stay away from junk food. It will give you zits." With that, Coach waved the girls away.

Outside, Meg walked to the curb and sat down to wait for Mom. *What a joke,* she thought, *prancing around, cheering for boys. Give me a break. Who's going to cheer for us?*

Mom pulled up in her big, green Buick. She waved a freshly manicured hand at Meg. "Meggie! How did it go?"

Meg yanked open the door and plopped into the passenger seat. "Like a mule in a pony show," she answered.

"Oh, so glad to hear it," Mom said as she patted Meg gingerly on her leg. "You look darling." Sometimes Mom just didn't get it. A mule in a pony show. Hmmph.

When they got home, Dad was lounging in his favorite armchair, doing a crossword puzzle.

"Our Meggie tried out for cheerleading tonight. Can you believe it?" She clicked her tongue to the roof of her mouth, clucking like a proud mother hen.

Dad looked up from his crossword puzzle. He raised a quizzical eyebrow at Meg. "You don't say, dear. You don't say."

Meg pushed her shoulders back and plastered a big wide smile across her face, just like she learned at cheerleading.

Mom pounced on Meg and squeezed her. "Oh, my little girl. Isn't she something!" Releasing Meg from her perfumed clutches, Mom said, "Let me go find more hair ribbons. Oh! And curlers! You can borrow my curlers anytime. I'll show you how to use them." She rushed up the stairs to her bedroom singing, "My little girl is becoming a woman!"

Meg rolled her eyes.

Dad pushed himself up from his recliner. He laid down the crossword puzzle on the coffee table and stood nose-to-nose with Meg.

"What are you scheming?"

Meg pretended to be all innocent. "I want to be a cheerleader. It's fun."

"Like Secretariat wants to be a cart horse." Dad wasn't buying it. "There's not a bone in your body that wants to strut around with pom-poms and wear ribbons in your hair. Why are you doing this to your mother? Just toying with her for fun?"

She felt guilty. She knew her parents, deep down, meant well. But her mother. Really, she was too much. Meg wished her mother would let her be.

"I just want to make Mom happy."

"For goodness sake, Meg. You're a teenager. No teenager wants to make their parents happy. What is going on? What are you plotting?"

Meg wavered. She'd never been very skilled at lying. Her face reflected her emotions like a clear mountain lake reflects moonlight. She half stomped her foot in frustration. Her emotions bubbled to the surface.

"Meg, baby," Dad moved in for a hug.

She pushed away. "I'm not a baby. I want to graduate and get away from all these kids. I want to go home—to Montana, where my friends get me."

"Honey," Dad tried to soothe her, "Home is here now. Time to put down roots." He wrapped his large arms around Meg, squeezing her to him, trying to make her feel safe, secure. "It was the right decision for us, for all of us." He rubbed her shoulders. "Aren't you glad we moved closer to Uncle Doc and Aunt Louise?"

Meg couldn't argue with that one. She was glad to have Uncle Doc and Aunt Louise in her life for real now, not casual mentions from a phone call or a letter. Calmer now, Meg decided to risk it and confide in her father. "Doc promised to take me and Tuck to New York to watch Ruffian run this spring." Meg paused, she'd wanted to choose her words carefully so her father would stay on her side but at the thought of Ruffian, the words poured out of her. "I thought if I did something for Mom, she'd do something for me and let me go with Doc."

"A-ha! I knew a horse had to be behind all of this."

"Don't tell Mom, please," she begged.

Dad studied her face. "I don't approve of you working people over to get what you want, especially your mother." Disappointment spread across his features. "I don't care whether or not you make some cheerleading squad. I want you to be honest and decent. You keep your grades up and no more of these mind games and we'll think about letting you go with Doc. You hear?"

Crestfallen, Meg went upstairs to her room. Dad was right. Playing games with people wasn't right. It made her no better than all of the other fake kids at her school who used people to get what they wanted. She felt like trash.

She dug into her hope chest and found her scrapbook. The last time she had added anything to it was the day she said goodbye to Ruffian. She read her entry from that page:

I have no one to talk to now that she's gone.

Underneath that sentence, she had taped a photograph of Ruffian standing in the wash rack.

Meg turned the page to a clean sheet. She ran her fingers over the empty page. *What next?* she wondered. *I am nothing special. No different than anyone else. I pretended to be something I'm not. Just to get on my mom's good side. I didn't want to hurt her. I just…I just…I don't know. What happened to me? To us?*

Closing her scrapbook, Meg wiped away a tear. She wrapped a mint green and yellow quilt around her body, nestling into it for comfort. It smelt of earth and alfalfa.

· · · · ·

Girls crowded around the bulletin board by the locker room. Coach had made her final decisions a day early. From down the hall, Meg could hear delighted squeals. Girls bounced up and down and clapped their hands in the air. Clearly, they had made the squad. Meg elbowed her way into the crowd, pulling her school books closer to her non-existent chest. The list was in alphabetical order and there, smack in the middle of the list, "Meg Murphy." *Oh dear Jesus.* Meg muttered, "I made the squad."

CHAPTER 13

Out of Control

Camden, South Carolina

February 1974

Back in South Carolina, Ruffian continued her training with Frank and his team. Nine o'clock in the morning and it was hot and muggy. "Gotta love the South," Frank Whiteley said, only partly to himself. Frank wiped his brow, readjusted his plaid shirt into his blue jeans, and positioned himself near the practice track's rails. A cigarette hung casually from his lips. He held a stopwatch in his right hand. His left hand was raised to signal the exercise jockey, Yates Kennedy, at the far turn on the track. Frank wanted to test out the Janney filly, the big black one with the fierce eyes, to see what potential she might have for the sport. He'd heard a lot of big talk from Nick and John back in Kentucky. Her training had gone pretty well since she came to Camden. But could she do well in a real race? A race with distance? It was time to see what this filly had. Was she ready for a maiden race?

Frank dropped his hand. Go! Yates gave the horse a whisper of a touch with his riding crop. Off flew the black filly. Her huge haunches pumped up and down, up and down, like pistons in a machine. Her long strides devoured yards in split seconds. Yates clung to the reins. As the filly barreled past Frank at the post, dirt and horse sweat hit him in the face.

"Three-eighths of a mile. Thirty-five and one-fifth for time," Frank shouted to Yates. The filly kept on running. "Get her under control man! Pull her up! Pull her up!" His shouts punctuated the early morning quiet.

Yates struggled to pull the monstrous horse to a stop. The horse wanted one thing: To run. The large filly jerked and sprung under Yates. She didn't want to give in. "Easy girl, easy. We're all done." Yates yanked the reins back harder, his biceps aching as he tried to bring the beast down to an even trot. "All. Done. Done," he said to the horse. The filly snorted and spat, angry at Yates for changing her flight plan.

"Have you ever seen anything like her?" Yates gasped to Frank as he approached the rail. Yates yanked the reins harder and harder again. Ruffian danced around in little circles, gradually slowing her pace, until finally giving way to Yates's command. Her eyes were white-rimmed. Steamy breath burst from her nostrils. "Hey, hey. She hates me for stopping her, don't she?" He pushed his goggles off his face. "She beat a record, didn't she, Frank?" Yates wiped track dirt from his face.

"Darn straight. Faster than Secretariat at that distance," Frank grinned. Before him stood a horse that might come around once in a lifetime, if a trainer was favored by the gods. Frank, modest and superstitious as he was, quickly hid his smile. "But my stopwatch might be wrong."

Yates laughed and shook his head. "Sure, boss, sure." Yates knew what he felt. This was no typical filly. On this filly, Yates felt like he was riding Pegasus, the winged horse of Zeus.

CHAPTER 14

Job Interview

April 1974

Yates, finished with another wild ride on Ruffian, hopped off her back and handed her off to Mike Bell, one of the assistant trainers at Frank's Camden, South Carolina, barn. Ruffian had worked hard on the training track again. Yates, and more importantly, Frank, were pleased with her speed and her work ethic. Besides, she had talent, beauty, and brains. A triple threat, the men joked amongst each other. Even covered with dirt, Ruffian looked majestic. Her deep brown eyes twinkled at Mike and Yates. She, too, was clearly pleased with her practice. She had beaten the sorrel colt in the one-mile practice race with ease.

Mike led her toward the wash racks for her bath. As Mike finished brushing out Ruffian's tail, she jumped forward in surprise. "Uh-uh, no way," he scolded her. "Stand still. No horseplay in this here barn." He continued running the brush through her tail.

"Excuse me, Mr. Bell?" The words got stuck in Meg's throat and came out all fragile sounding. Ruffian lifted her nose and nickered to Meg. Then she buried her face in Meg's hands, running her large forehead affectionately up and down against

Meg's fingernails.

"That's me," Mike answered, slightly puzzled at his horse's friendly behavior with this girl. He took his ball cap off and scratched his balding head.

"I'm, um, I'm Meg Murphy."

Mike raised an eyebrow, "So?"

"I used to work with Ruffian back in Kentucky. Mr. Whiteley, um, I called him last week, and asked about a job here." Meg stuttered. "He said he might have one and I should talk to you." She added, "Sir," hoping to sound polite.

Mike set the brush down and motioned for Meg to follow him. They went outside.

"Take a seat," Mike instructed, pointing to a pair of lawn chairs up against the shed in the cool shade of the oak trees. "How old are you?" Mike narrowed his eyes.

"Sixteen."

"You in school?"

"I was. In Kentucky. Junior year of high school."

"Did you drop out to chase horses? Or worse, men?"

"No sir," Meg was at a loss for words. "Never, sir. No way…" she grappled for words, embarrassed by Mike's questions. How could she explain to Mike Bell how phenomenal Ruffian was to her?

"Then, Miss, I don't understand at all what you are thinking. Or what you are doing here."

"Mr. Bell, I came to South Carolina with Doc. To see if I might work for you and for Mr. Whiteley. If you hire me, I promise, sir, I will enroll in school and finish out the year here."

"Are you a runaway?" Mike was used to runaways trying to find work at race tracks, getting paid in cash, trying to stay off law enforcement's radar.

"No, sir. I swear. Doc is my uncle. My dad's brother who err who..." *You're sounding like a fool, Megan Murphy, stop running your mouth, why would Mike Bell of all people need to know your whole convoluted family tree?*

Mike was silent. Meg knew he was studying her, trying to determine if she was lying.

"Mr. Bell, my mother agreed to let me do this—on the condition that I live with my aunt and uncle here in Camden since they're working for Frank here.... And I promise to earn my high school diploma." Meg reached into her pocket. She handed Mike a piece of paper. It read:

> *Suzanne Murphy, mother to Megan Murphy, of Lexington, Kentucky, telephone number 555-7508. I give my permission for Meg to live with my sister-in-law Louise Murphy in Camden, South Carolina, and enroll in public high school. Please telephone me if you have any questions.*
>
> *Sincerely,*
>
> *Suzanne Murphy*

Mike looked up from the typed sheet of paper. "Let me call this number and run it by the legal team. And Doc." He narrowed his eyes. But Meg didn't flinch. She wasn't lying. She had nothing to hide from him. Everything was legit. "Even if you are who you say you are, why would I hire a girl with a cast on her arm? What good are you?"

Meg glanced at her right arm. "It'll be off in two more weeks. Then I'll be good as new."

"How'd you break it?"

"Cheerleading."

"A cheerleader. Just what we need around here." Mike shook his head.

"I'm not a cheerleader," Meg stammered. "Well, not technically."

"From the looks of you, you weren't a very good one." A smile spread across Mike's face.

"Fair enough, sir. I can't argue with that. I caused the whole pyramid to fall down during our first scrimmage game. I was lucky it was just one broken arm." Meg didn't want to be reminded of her graceless days as a cheerleader. Those days were behind her. After the pyramid accident, her mother realized Meg would never be the popular, perky girl she'd always hoped for. While Meg was recuperating after the fall, all she did was mope around the house, and talk on and on about horses and getting back to the barn. She practically drove her mother mad. Nobody at school wanted to ride or even talk about horses—not even Sarah and Eliza. It was all about dating, partying, cars, fashion, dieting. Meg's grades were falling. She'd lost interest in her classes. Her mother said she was "languishing."

"Let her come with us—to South Carolina. Time with us and the horses will do her more good than you can imagine," Aunt Louise said to Mom and Dad one evening over supper. "She can help us out and Frank's team, too."

"It's so far away," Mom fidgeted with her fingernails. "What if…"

"Suzanne, it's a day's drive. That's all."

"What about school?"

"We'll get her enrolled in Camden. And we'll keep her busy at the barn so she can't get into any trouble. Doc will see to it."

"It doesn't seem right shipping my daughter off for someone else to raise."

"You ain't shipping her off. You're sending her with family."

Mom choked back tears. "I know she and I haven't seen eye to eye on a lot of things lately."

"Suzanne, let us help you out. Meg is going through a rough patch. I think the horses can pull her out of it."

Mom pushed the pot roast around her plate, stirring the meat into the mashed potatoes. "A change of scenery couldn't hurt," her mother conceded. "I want to see my girl happy. Whatever that looks like for her."

It couldn't have worked out any better if Meg had cooked this scheme up herself. She was back with Uncle Doc and Aunt Louise. Most of all, she had a slim chance to be back with Ruffian, who was finishing her race training with Frank.

"Please, Mr. Bell, here's my Aunt Louise's phone number. You may call me there. If you want to hire me, sir," Meg handed Mike another slip of paper with a Camden address and phone number. "Or talk to Doc, your vet," she added. "He'll vouch for me. I'm a hard worker."

Mike stood up. He offered his hand to Meg. "Nice to meet you, Miss Murphy. I'll think about it." Meg knew it was her cue to leave. Mike had given her enough of his valuable time. A firm handshake and it was all over, her one shot at being with Ruffian again.

As she walked away a loud, other-worldly screech rang out from the barn. Meg turned on her heels and bolted back into the barn. Still tied in the wash rack with just one lead rope, Ruffian had managed to get herself twisted up in the metal chain. It was wrapped around her neck.

"Shshhh, girl, settle down," Meg whispered to Ruffian. "You got yourself all tangled up when our backs were turned." Ruffian's eyes were wide with panic. She pawed at the rubber mats in the wash rack, squealing. Meg slipped next to Ruffian and quickly unclipped her halter from the metal chain. With the tension released, Ruffian's breathing settled. Meg stroked her neck. Mike, wheezing and out of breath from running from the far side of the barn, doubled over in front of Meg and Ruffian. "What the heck," he gasped.

"No worries, sir. Ruffian got bored and found herself some trouble." Meg reassured Mike, "She's all right."

Mike caught his breath. "I like how calm you are, kid. I like how you handled this situation."

"Thank you, sir."

"Tell you what? I'll see Doc in the morning and I'll speak to him about you. 'Til then, how about you put Ruffian back in her stall. I've got tack that needs cleaning. You can do that with one good arm, can't you?"

Meg, delighted, bounced up and down, spooking Ruffian and causing her to dance a jig, too. "Yes, sir!" Meg squealed. For the first time ever, she felt like a cheerleader.

CHAPTER 15

Horse People

"Don't worry, Mom. Aunt Louise makes sure I eat my vegetables," Meg spoke into the telephone. She twirled the beige telephone cord in her fingers, imagining the phone cord as reins for Ruffian.

Mom's anxious voice replied, "And school? How's it going? Make any friends?"

"It's okay, I guess."

"Okay?"

"Yeah. Biology is pretty cool. I've been staying after school to help set up the labs for the next day with the teacher."

"That's nice." Mom paused. "Do you want to be a teacher someday?"

Meg answered bluntly, "Not really. I don't like teenagers. She's just cool, you know? We talk about animals and cells and medicine. Said she always wanted to be a doctor, but her family told her that girls couldn't be doctors."

Mom replied with a polite, "Um-hmm."

"Course that was in the 1950s so things have changed. Mrs. Reed likes teaching though."

"Well, dear, keep your grades up. And if you do, it's fine with me if you tag along to the barn with your Uncle Doc every now and then."

Meg's eyes darted to the wall calendar above the kitchen table. She'd been in South Carolina for three weeks and she'd been at the barn with Doc every day but one—and that was for Aunt Louise's birthday. Meg thought it best not to mention how frequently she was there. As long as her grades were good and she ate her vegetables, Mom would be happy. If Mom was happy, Meg might be able to stay in South Carolina with Ruffian even longer. Permanently, maybe. She'd prove that she is responsible.

Doc came into the kitchen from the garage. He had a stack of file folders in his arms.

"Gotta go, Mom. Love you."

"Uh, love you too, dear."

Meg hung up the telephone. She moved her math textbook off the kitchen table so Doc would have room to put his folders down.

"Hey, there, kiddo? How was school?"

"Fine."

"Those Southern Belles getting to you?"

"Nah. I'm used to them."

Doc pulled out a kitchen chair and sat down. He looked Meg in the eyes. She recognized that look. It was the same look he used when he examined a horse. He was searching deep down to determine what precisely was going on. "It ain't easy to pull up your roots and move to a new place."

"I like it here, Doc. With you and Aunt Louise and the horses."

"It is a different kind of life though. Not much time or money for stuff besides the horses."

"I don't mind."

"You making friends?"

"Why does everyone keep asking me that?" Meg sighed.

Doc chuckled. "Well, are you?"

"I guess so. I sit with a couple of girls at lunch. We're in biology and calculus together."

Doc sorted through his folders as Meg talked.

"Sarah and Eliza. Sarah wants to be a dentist and Eliza wants to be a chiropractor. They're the ones who told me about helping Mrs. Reed right after school." Meg's voice trailed off. Doc looked up from his folders. Meg fumbled. Dang it. There was no fooling Doc. She knew that he knew those were the names of her only two friends back in Kentucky. He had caught her in her story.

"What do you want to do after high school?" He asked her, choosing to take no notice of her tall tale.

"I guess I thought I'd just work at the barn."

"But?" Doc urged her.

"Science is interesting. Hard but interesting."

"I enjoyed it," Doc added. "It was one thing in school that interested me besides woodworking class."

Meg tilted her head. She began to see Doc. Doc as a boy, Doc dealing with teachers and grades and friends.

"Meg, I don't like to tell people how to live their lives but I will tell you this: Do what you love. Don't worry about what nobody else thinks of you. Oh, and eat your vegetables."

Meg rolled her eyes at Doc and giggled. He knew her mother.

Oh so well.

"Want to review these charts with me? We're getting ready to give the next round of vaccinations and dewormers to the horses." Doc opened a folder. In his clear, precise handwriting Meg saw the horse's name, birthdate, and vitals. She saw the list of medications and vaccines the horse had six months ago. All of its biological history, right there, in Doc's manila folder.

When Aunt Louise came home from the grocery store two hours later, Meg and Doc were just finishing with the folders. Aunt Louise had three large paper bags. "Watch out, I'm heading straight to that table." Aunt Louise, lean and long like a Thoroughbred, swayed toward them. Her paper bags were chock-full of food.

"I'm famished," Meg said, watching Aunt Louise plant the bags onto the table.

"You are in luck. Fresh bologna, fresh cheese. Warm up the skillet!" Aunt Louise laughed.

Doc jumped up, turned on the gas burner, and slid the cast iron skillet onto the flame. He dropped a generous pat of butter into the skillet. Meg licked her lips. Her stomach growled. Doc buttered thick slices of white bread and layered thick cut bologna and cheese between the bread. The skillet sizzled as Doc set the bologna and cheese sandwiches on the hot cast iron.

Meg moved their folders and set the table while Aunt Louise unloaded the rest of the groceries. Theirs was a cozy home, Meg thought. Easy, straightforward. You put in a good day's work and you sit down to a simple meal with those you love. What more could a person ask for? No fuss.

"Sandwiches are hot and ready!" Doc said. With a spatula, he slid a sandwich on each of the three paper plates.

Meg bit into her sandwich. Gooey American cheese trailed out from the bread.

"Almost forgot the vegetables!" Doc winked at Meg. "Add some onions to your sandwiches. Have a glass of tomato juice." He went to the refrigerator, grabbed the sliced onions, and poured V-8 juice for everyone.

How could families be so different? Meg wondered. At her parents' house, they had a full dinner every night—meat, potatoes, veggies— in their proper dining room, on their good china no less. At Doc and Aunt Louise's place, they whipped up a no fuss dinner and plopped down at the kitchen table. Sometimes they didn't eat dinner until eight or nine o'clock at night, depending on what had happened at the barn that day. Paper plates were the norm here. Her mother would keel over and die if she ever found out how often they ate TV dinners.

When the trio finished their bologna sandwiches, Doc headed to the bathroom to shower off from his day. Meg lingered in the kitchen. Aunt Louise rinsed the skillet and wiped the grease off the stove top. She filled the sink with hot water and dish soap.

"Thanks for supper," Meg said as she leaned against the kitchen counter, watching her aunt wash the glasses and cereal bowls from the morning.

"No problem," Louise smiled at Meg. "It's nice having you around."

"My mom thinks I'm hopeless."

Aunt Louise set her dish rag down and turned to face Meg.

Meg went on, "She just doesn't get it. Horses, I mean. That's all I want."

"Can I tell you something?"

Meg nodded.

"There are normal people and then there are horse people. Horse people eat, breathe, sleep, and dream horses. There's nothing else in the world besides horses." Aunt Louise winked at Meg. "Know any folks like that?"

Meg did. They were Doc and Aunt Louise and Nick and Mike and Yates and Frank Whiteley. Her horse people. They smelled of the land. Dust and dirt caked their jeans and shoes. Bumps and bruises painted their arms and legs. Horse people.

"Normal people don't ever understand horse people and you got to just accept it and keep on doing your thing, as long as it makes you happy."

Doc came down the stairs with wet hair and a clean t-shirt and trousers. "Whoa, why are my gals looking so darn serious?"

"Talking horses, that's all," Aunt Louise said and finished drying the dishes.

CHAPTER 16

The Jockey

It had been a busy day of deworming and vaccinating. Meg tagged along behind Doc, taking the used needles and disposing of them as he went from horse to horse. Ruffian fussed a tad when Doc stuck the dewormer syringe down her throat. She reeled back and flung her head left and right. Doc scolded her like a toddler. "Don't you be such a pig-headed baby. This here medicine is gonna keep you strong and healthy as an ox."

At the word "ox," as if she was somehow offended, Ruffian squealed and tried to rear. Luckily, Meg had already tied her up in the wash rack. There was a long metal chain attached to each wall that also clipped onto each side of her halter, preventing Ruffian from bolting away.

Doc got all the medicine into Ruffian. "She's the last one," he said as he passed Meg the used needles and syringe. "Think she deserves a treat?" Doc patted Ruffian's withers.

"Of course she does. Got to teach her there's nothing to be afraid of. Doctors only want to help her." Meg reached into her pants pocket and offered Ruffian a peppermint candy. Ruffian greedily gummed Meg's hand. "Hey! Watch the fingers!" Meg laughed at the hungry horse.

"Let's put her back in her stall and load up. I hear tomorrow they're bringing the real jock to the barn to ride. Don't want to miss that, do you?" he asked.

Ruffian did a sidestep as Meg unclipped her from the wash rack. She was eager to get back to her stall to finish her supper. But a thousand-pound dancing animal was a red flag of danger in a barn. Meg yanked the lead rope hard, straight down. "Set-tuhl-DOWN," Meg said as she popped the lead rope, pulling Ruffian's head down with three terse jerks. "Do not act like a monster. You have manners. I know. I taught them to you." Ruffian, now in check, followed behind Meg to the stall, giving little snorts like a scolded child.

"That's a good girl. You have class. Remember that." Meg stroked Ruffian's forehead. Ruffian lowered her large head to Meg's chest. Her brown eyes were now at eye level with Meg's. "Kiss-kiss," Meg puckered her lips. Ruffian bumped her lips ever so gently to Meg's. "Love you," Meg said as she slid the stall door closed. Ruffian nickered in reply.

Meg turned and found Doc sitting on the lawn chair across the alley. He had his handkerchief to his face, wiping something out of his eyes. Meg blushed. How long had her uncle been sitting there? She was sure the real grooms never made their racehorses give them a "kiss-kiss." She was lucky Frank or Tuck or Nick hadn't been there to see her. Good grief, how they would tease her. Meg decided to pretend that nothing had happened and that she hadn't acted like a big softie to a racehorse.

"All set. I'm ready to head home," she said to Doc, wiping her dirty hands on her jeans.

Doc drove the pickup down the highway, heading back into

Camden. He liked to listen to country western music on the way home, especially Jeannie C. Riley. Her song "Harper Valley PTA" was playing on the radio. "It's relaxing," he told Meg before he started singing along.

As the song faded on the airwaves, Meg interrupted her uncle's serenade. "Who's the jock they're bringing in tomorrow?"

Doc, his eyes never leaving the road, answered, "Jacinto Vasquez."

"Don't know him."

"Frank's been talking to him about riding. Jacinto has been in some trouble, been suspended. But Frank still wants him."

"Wants him for who?"

"Ruffian."

Meg saw how well Ruffian had been working during her practice races. She thought the horse had a gift. She knew Frank Whiteley saw it. Heck, everyone saw it. Except nobody wanted to get too excited about Ruffian's speed, for fear she might pull a muscle or worse. Horse racing was a superstitious business. Misfortune favored the fortunate, as Frank had told her.

"Frank's going to put Jacinto on Ruffian and see what he can do. Can't wait to see a pro jockey ride her." Doc turned his truck, heading for home. Chuckling deep from his belly, he added, "Course, it is going to be even more interesting to see those two hard- headed men try to work together."

After a supper of boxed mashed potatoes and ham and cheese sandwiches, Meg went into the den to do her English homework. Her writing prompt for this week's essay on "Character" was: "Love is one of the greatest human capabilities. What does it mean to love someone?" On Doc's typewriter, she wrote:

To love someone means to accept them for who they are. Not for who you want them to be. Not for who you hope they will become. For who they are, right here, right now. No matter what.

It is generally expected that parents love their children. For example, my parents are caring and they are responsible. My mom doesn't work outside our home. My dad is a banker. He works a lot so he can provide for my mom and me. He wants us to have a comfortable life because he did not have a comfortable life growing up. Even though I know they love me (and I love them), they are pushing me to settle down and become someone's wife right after high school. All I want to do is work with horses. I don't want to get married, at least not for a long time. They say they love me and say they want what's best for me. But I need to decide for myself what makes me happy.

Another example of love is my Uncle Doc and his wife Louise. They love each other and they love me. He is a vet. Aunt Louise works in the vet clinic for him. She does the books and manages the appointments. They are a great team. They work hard but always laugh and joke with each other. Now that I'm living with them, I am happier. I miss my mom and dad but I don't have that pressure on me to become someone I'm not. My aunt and uncle are cool with me tagging along and doing horse stuff. I feel that my parents and my aunt and uncle love me, just in very different ways. I once thought that maybe you could only love someone if they were exactly like you, like the same beliefs or personality or whatever. But that belief changed last year when I met the love of my life.

The biggest love in my life is this brown-eyed beauty. She is huge and graceful, and feisty. She is a racehorse and I get to work with her after school. I groom her, muck out her stall, feed her, and clean her tack. I get to watch her do her practice races. When I'm having a rough day, she cheers me up. She'll give me kisses or act silly. I feel like this horse loves me and understands me. She doesn't care about my grades, my clothes, my future. She just likes having me around. That is love.

There are many kinds of love. Parents have love for their children. Sometimes they hope and expect too much though. Sometimes they push too hard. They forget to stop worrying about the future. But maybe their worrying is a form of love? Love also exists between humans and animals. Even though we don't speak the same language, the animals we care for love us—and I love them—no matter what.

Midnight. Meg rubbed her eyes. She unrolled the paper from the typewriter. After skimming the page for any misspellings, she tucked it into her backpack for Monday morning. *Done,* she exhaled. It was scattered but passable. *Now I can concentrate on this weekend at the barn.* She looked forward to meeting a real professional jockey. She'd heard stories about professional jockeys that floated around the barn. They had a certain reputation. Fast living, hard drinking, women chasing, fearless, tough as tacks. They gambled on everything, including life, people said. Where some folks might think these were negative character traits, Meg thought of it as part of the job requirements. Really, it would take guts to perch yourself on the back of a racehorse. Death could meet you at any step. Besides, meeting a professional jockey only meant one thing: Frank thinks Ruffian has what it takes to go to the big races.

• • • • •

Near the practice track, Frank towered over a small Spanish man. The Spanish man squinted his eyes at Frank, clearly not happy about the arrangement. Meg couldn't hear what was being said but she knew Frank didn't back down from his plans. She walked across the dirt lane up to Frank, and waited for his orders.

"Jacinto, I tell you, this filly has spark. She could whip the pants right off any two-year-old colt out there."

Jacinto tilted his head to consider Frank's statement. "Run her with the big dogs then, Frank. Prove it. Run her with the colts." There was more money and prestige in the colt races, at least that's what most people thought. Colts tended to be larger and faster than the fillies.

"Nah. I don't believe in racing 'em together. Most of the time it just ain't fair to the fillies to burn 'em out so young. Ruins their bones." Frank rubbed his forehead, a sign that he was tiring of the discussion at hand. "This one, though, can go far with the fillies. She looks to me like the fastest filly in the world." Frank stopped and this time he narrowed his eyes at the small Hispanic man, "Want to be part of this or don't you, Vasquez?"

Jacinto placed his hands on his hips. "Show me what you got, Frank."

Frank turned to Meg. He barked, "Get Ruffian saddled for Mr. Vasquez. Hurry it up."

"Yes, sir," Meg said, rushing back toward the barn.

Meg brushed Ruffian's coat and picked her hooves clean as fast as she could. Ruffian neighed at Meg and pawed at the floor. Meg knew her own nervous electricity was agitating Ruffian, who drew in a deep breath and quivered. The horse felt electric, too. Time to run.

On the practice track, Ruffian high stepped. Meg could hardly hold the horse. Jacinto stood by the rail, examining Ruffian's movements.

Frank shouted to Meg, "Walk her around. Let him see her strut her stuff."

Meg led Ruffian past Jacinto, toward the starting boxes. Ruffian flicked her ears forward and lifted her regal nose in the air, her hooves dancing across the dirt.

"Ay! That's enough," Jacinto waved at Meg. "Bring her back to me."

"You like what you see?" Frank asked slyly. "Is she as good as those horses you rode down in Mexico?"

"Panama," Jacinto corrected Frank. "*Jesu Cristo,* you white guys can't never get it right. I'm from Panama, Frank, once and for all. Panama." Jacinto turned to walk away from Frank. He spat at Meg, "I ain't going to ride for some hick trainer who thinks all us Spanish speakers are the same."

"Mr. Vasquez, Mr. Whiteley ain't like that, sir…wait," Meg holding Ruffian's reins, fumbled for the words. She didn't want Frank's harsh words to cause Jacinto to walk out and not take the job. They needed someone fearless, someone intense. Someone whose swagger could match Ruffian's. They needed Jacinto Vasquez. "I think he's messing with you, sir. He does that to folks. He tests them to see what they can handle."

Jacinto looked Meg resolutely in the eyes. "I don't take no disrespect. From no one."

"Yes, sir. Got it." His calculated stare sent shivers down Meg's spine. She could see how this man could control a thousand-pound animal galloping at full throttle in a field full of horses. Jacinto Vasquez was tough.

Frank cleared his throat. "Ah, Vasquez, the girl's onto me. I'm messing with you. Settle down, son. I'm offering you a fine horse. A horse that might come along once in a lifetime—for any jock."

Jacinto's mouth twisted in consternation. "She's a beauty. I give you that, Frank. I want to feel her run before I agree to anything."

Ruffian lifted her nose toward Jacinto and nickered. "I think she's up for your challenge," Meg told Jacinto.

"It is up to her, is it?" he asked.

"For this one, yes," Meg replied. "You'll see what I mean."

Frank gave Jacinto a hand to get up into the saddle.

"You sure this one is a filly, Frank? She's as big as a tank."

Jacinto gathered the reins in his hands as Meg unclipped the lead rope. "I'll take her out for a spin." Jacinto clicked his tongue in his cheeks and pressed his legs into Ruffian's sides. Ruffian sprang forward. They were off.

The dirt flew from under Ruffian's hooves. Jacinto crouched on her back. He looked small and as still as a marble statue even though they were moving at top speed. Ruffian stretched out long and lean at the gallop. Around the quarter mile mark, the half, and into the homestretch. She sailed past the finish line. Jacinto gave her the cue and she slowed to the canter, a big, wide-rolling canter, like riding a rocking horse. With the slightest of pulls on her reins, Jacinto brought her to a trot on the far side of the track. He gave her plenty of time to slow and cool down.

Frank said to Meg, "Think he believes me now?"

"I betcha he's never felt anything like her."

"She's the biggest thing I've ever seen. And to move at those speeds! Bet that surprised him! When I called him on the phone, he told me she sounds like a tank! Ha!" He laughed.

Frank grinned at Meg, "It's mighty fun to surprise folks sometimes, isn't it? Give them what they least expected."

Meg felt proud of her filly and of the work their team had done to bring Ruffian to this point. She was a world-class athlete, a superstar, and she hadn't even run a real race yet. It was getting time for her to show the world how special she was.

"Go help him off her," Frank said, pointing toward the high-stepping filly.

Meg dashed from Frank's side. She needed to cross the track and gather Ruffian from Jacinto to finish cooling Ruffian out.

As Meg approached the horse and rider, Jacinto's expression startled her. Jacinto's eyes sparkled. He looked euphoric like a gladiator who had just won a battle. Meg reached up to grab the reins from him and help him off Ruffian. He laughed at Meg, "Ole Mr. Whiteley better let no one but me ride her."

"Isn't she something?" Meg asked him as he hopped off the horse.

"Something isn't the right word for her, kid. She is magic. Pure magic."

Ruffian neighed and kicked up her back legs.

"I think so, too," Meg said in Ruffian's ear as she walked the horse toward Frank. "You are my Miss Magic."

Approaching Frank at the rail, Jacinto puffed out his chest and said, "Frank, you got yourself a deal. I'll ride your tank-butt filly. Whenever you need me."

Frank laughed heartily and slapped Jacinto on the back. "I thought you'd appreciate her."

"I've never met a filly like her," Jacinto said as he wiped the sweat from his forehead.

Frank took a puff on his cigarette, "Keep your calendar clear this spring, Jacinto. We're going to the races."

The trio walked the horse back to the stables with hope in their hearts, savoring the smell of horse sweat and pine trees.

CHAPTER 17

Chica in Trouble

Camden, South Carolina

May 1974

Meg cantered Ruffian on the practice track. Jacinto and Frank had a big meeting planned and they had asked Meg to give Ruffian's legs a little stretch. Nothing too wild, Jacinto said, just a light lope around the track. Meg had wasted no time grabbing her helmet and saddling Ruffian. It wasn't everyday they let her ride. Most of the time, the guys got to ride. Even in the real races, they didn't let many women ride. Diane Crump and Barbara Jo Rubin were but two female jockeys in an industry of men. Meg didn't think it was fair really. Why were men any different from her? She'd been riding for a while and doing everything else around the barn, yet she still hadn't become an official exercise rider. She'd said something to Frank about it once. He kind of shrugged Meg off, telling her that the boys could handle broken ribs and hips. So when they'd told her to exercise Ruffian today, Meg was surprised, to say the least. She had Ruffian out to the practice track before you could say "SecretariartwontheTripleCrown."

One, two, three, one, two, three, one, two, three, Meg chanted to herself as Ruffian rolled through the canter. Her canter was large, steady, rolling, like a wave making its way to shore. Yet underneath Meg moved a thousand-pound animal that could easily spook and run away with her. Or worse, kill her with one wrong move. Meg trusted Frank's meticulous training but she'd seen many a well-broke horse spook at a bird flying past or at a car's horn. Meg's left hand lifted to check her helmet. *It's snug, good,* Meg thought. She smiled to herself, remembering the barn's motto, "Safety first." She relaxed in the saddle, lowering her hands closer to Ruffian's neck, extending her heels deep into the stirrups. Meg could not help smiling as the breeze brushed her face. *This is what flying would feel like,* Meg mused. How she wished she could ride in a real race—with Ruffian. No one but the wind would touch them. *Pegasus,* Meg whispered.

Meg inched her hands slightly forward. Ruffian felt the cue and slid from the rolling canter into a gallop. Meg felt air underneath Ruffian. Then she felt air between her and the saddle. Ruffian, eager to go even faster, extended her neck. Meg felt her body sliding out from under her. She tried to gather her legs under her, trying to wrap her own body around Ruffian's. Just air. Hoofbeats. Air. *Onetwothreefouronetwothreefour.* Air. The horse was moving too swiftly. Meg held her breath. She slid to the right of the saddle. She saw dirt. And braced herself for impact. But then Ruffian eased her pace. Just enough for Meg to pull herself up and get ahold of the reins. "Whoa, girl," Meg said as loud and forcefully as she could. "Whoa!" Ruffian snorted at the command. "Whoa. Whoa!" This time Ruffian slowed. Meg, catching her breath, guided Ruffian back down into the canter.

Coming around the far stretch, Meg saw Jacinto jogging

toward the rail.

"Chica!" Jacinto yelled. "Chica!"

Ruffian and Meg were almost neck to neck with Jacinto. He shouted at them, "Pull her up. What are you doing? You crazy? You no exercise jock! She carry you away!"

Meg waved to Jacinto to signal that she heard him. She cooed to Ruffian, "Whoa, whoa." Ruffian snorted. She didn't want to stop moving. "Whoa," Meg said again. This time Ruffian begrudgingly slowed her pace to a bouncy trot. Meg cooled her down, slowly easing her to a walk.

"Good girl," she said as she patted Ruffian's neck. "A light workout before your supper." She knew now what it felt like to ride the wind—terrifying but glorious at the same time. Ruffian flicked her ears at the word "supper." This horse never skipped a meal.

She hopped off and led Ruffian to the barn. Jacinto and Frank were waiting for them. Frank's brow was wrinkled, his eyes dark. Jacinto must have just told Frank about her taking Ruffian to the gallop—against Frank's training instructions.

"Think you're a big shot jock now, kid?" Frank asked.

Meg, worried that Frank might fire her, froze. Jacinto jumped in. "Hey, Frank, she's gonna be too tall to be a jock. Look at her. She's eye to eye with me now and she's still got growing to do."

"I wish I could be a jockey. Jacinto is probably right though. I'll be taller than him before summer comes."

"Hey, easy there, chica," Jacinto replied, "Dynamite comes in small packages." Jacinto lifted up both arms and flexed his muscles.

"Glad you two have time to joke around when we got this here horse to load in the morning," Frank reminded them. "We've got packing to do. And Meg, I don't need no kid getting killed around my barn. No more galloping. You hear?"

Meg choked out an obedient "Yes, sir."

"Yeah, yeah, Frank. All work and no play," Jacinto said. He liked to poke Frank. It was a little like playing cat and mouse, but with a grizzly bear.

The barn door swung open, interrupting their sparring. There stood Tuck. Proud as a stallion just finished in the breeding shed. His arms were loaded with brown paper bags.

"Dinner is served!" Tuck sang as he entered the barn. Doc came in after him, carrying five Styrofoam cups of soda. Tuck unpacked the bagged dinner on a tack box, spreading napkins out so their food wouldn't get dusty.

"Good to see you again, young man," Frank said. "Thanks for bringing supper, too."

Meg, starving from the intense exercise gallop, eyed the picnic dinner. She licked her lips. Frank saw her. "You gonna put that horse away or you gonna give her our fried chicken?"

Ruffian whinnied as if to remind Meg about her own supper. "I didn't forget you," Meg whispered to her. "Looks like I'll be the last one to dinner. Hope those guys save me some."

When Meg got Ruffian in her stall, she slid off the saddle and unclipped the bridle. Meg turned to walk out of the stall with the tack. "Stay put. Don't go anywhere," she told Ruffian. Just as she stepped out of the doorway and bent over to set the saddle and bridle on the rack, Ruffian bolted.

"Craaapppppp!!!!!!!!!!!!" Meg yelled as Ruffian skittered toward Tuck.

Jacinto jumped from his lawn chair, "What the--!"

"For Chrissake!" shouted Frank.

Tuck cowered over his picnic spread on the tack box, protecting its sacred contents from the loose horse.

Ruffian swerved right, ducking her head under Tuck's arm. Tuck fell backwards. Ruffian jerked her head up. A cornbread muffin hung from her mouth. She swallowed it in one gulp.

Doc slapped his hands on his thighs, "Not Louise's homemade muffins! Those are my favorites!"

Meg swooped in front of Ruffian, grabbed her by the nose. "Toss me that halter," she barked. Tuck threw one to her. In a swift sweep of her arms, Meg had the halter over Ruffian's ears and clipped it tight. She shook her finger in Ruffian's face. "I told you to stay put, you rascal." Ruffian licked her lips unapologetically.

Frank scolded Meg, "What kind of two-bit pony show do you think we run around here? Get that horse put away. Right this time."

Meg knew better than to argue with the boss, especially today. She'd messed up twice. Her relaxed attitude with Ruffian could have gotten someone hurt. Ruffian wasn't some kid's backyard pony after all. She was a hot- blooded racehorse.

When she returned to the men, she found most of the fried chicken gone. They'd left her a drumstick, a muffin, and a half a cup of baked beans. *Better than nothing,* she thought. Frank had laid out a list of supplies to load. Doc brought Ruffian's vaccination paperwork for the journey to New York.

Frank said, "We're leaving at six am sharp. So we load the trailer tonight. For yerselfs, bring four days' worth of track clothes and one nice Sunday outfit in case we win and get invited to a swanky party. Meg, you might want to see about a dress, just in case."

Embarrassed to be pointed out among all these men, she blushed and looked down at her boots.

Doc added, "Tuck came up from Kentucky. He's riding along to be an extra set of hands. There's going to be a lot of commotion with all those people. We need to put familiar people around Ruffian—to keep her head on straight."

Meg thought she could see Tuck's chest puff out like a proud old peacock. Jacinto leaned into Tuck, "You do a good job and maybe Frank'll have you riding in the next stakes race."

"There's nothing I'd rather do," Tuck answered. "I'll ride anything you got, Mr. Whiteley. Anything. And I mean it."

Meg felt a surge of jealousy pulse through her. *He'll be a jockey as soon as he's legal age,* she thought. *And nobody'll blink twice.* Meg, on the other hand, knew she would be expected to give up horses and the track to settle down and get married. She'd have to start acting like a lady and start popping out babies. At least, according to Mom.

"You're getting ahead of yourself, kid," Frank pointed out. "You got a lot of learning to do before any of that pans out."

She smiled in triumph. Maybe Frank won't make it so easy for Tuck after all. Tuck would have to work from the bottom and prove himself like all the other jockeys had. *That would be democratic,* Meg thought, *highly democratic.*

Later, as Meg was packing the blankets, Tuck plopped himself on a bale of alfalfa.

"Hear that? Frank might let me be one of his jockeys."

"Um-hmm. Maybe one day."

"Then you can say, 'I knew him when.'"

"When he was humble."

"That's plain mean, Meg."

"Why would Frank choose you over anyone else?"

Tuck answered confidently, "Cuz, I'm Doc's nephew."

"I'm his niece," Meg reminded Tuck.

"Sure, but it's different."

"How?"

"You're a girl. Girls don't ride in the real races."

"Times are changing, Tuck." She'd seen it in the newspapers. Women were breaking barriers, like Billie Jean King smashing records in tennis, proving that it wasn't a 'man's game' after all. Meg thought back to a conversation she had with her mother on the phone the week before. Again, her mother had extolled the virtues of homemaking and settling down with a man after graduation. She'd told Meg there was nothing wrong with a safe, comfortable life. Meg bristled. Why couldn't her mother change with the times? Why was she stuck in the 1950s? Why did Tuck sound like he was stuck in the '50s, too? "We women can do whatever we want."

"Oh yeah, sure. You might stay an exercise rider. Or marry a jock. But you won't have a real job like me."

Meg threw a bell boot at Tuck's face. It hit him squarely on the nose. "What do you know!"

"Ouch! Chill out." Tuck rubbed his nose and checked for blood. "That's why you'll never be a pro—women are hysterical."

Ruffian pawed at the bedding in her stall. Restless. Agitated.

She threw the other bell boot at Tuck. It hit his chest. "Open your mouth again, and you'll get a pair of clippers thrown at ya."

Tuck dashed away. "Hysterical woman!" he shouted as he ran.

"Stupid boy," she grumbled. "He doesn't know what I can or cannot do."

Ruffian nickered.

CHAPTER 18

On the Road

Meg's bags were packed for New York. Late the night before, Aunt Louise lent Meg one of her polyester dresses, a red one, to match Ruffian's racing silks, a pair of nylon pantyhose, and a pair of ballet flats. Aunt Louise even let Meg borrow her favorite red Avon lipstick. She wanted Meg to look like a real knockout at any after-race event. Aunt Louise had giggled like a school girl as Meg packed her suitcase, talking about seeing all the famous jockeys and trainers.

Dawn hadn't yet crept up over the horizon as Meg shoveled scrambled eggs into her mouth. Aunt Louise and Doc nursed their morning coffees.

Aunt Louise, winking at Meg, said to Doc, "Don't let any of those wild horsemen take a shine to our Meg."

"I won't let her out of my sight."

"I don't have time for boys," Meg added, "I've got a racehorse to look after."

"Horsemen can be charming when they want to," Aunt Louise said as she pecked Doc on the cheek and got up to clean the plates off the table.

Meg, with a mouth full of eggs, replied, "Not half as charming as Ruffian."

"Keep thinking that way—at least for another ten years," Doc said as he grinned at Aunt Louise.

Meg spooned the last of the scrambled eggs into her mouth and gulped down her glass of milk. "It's time to head out," Meg pointed to the clock on the kitchen wall. 5:30am. She couldn't wait to get to Belmont Park for Ruffian's maiden race. She couldn't wait to show the world Ruffian. To show the world the fastest filly. The fastest horse ever born.

Doc drove his truck down the lane toward the barn. Meg could see headlights near the barn door. Shadows of people darted in between the beams of light.

Tuck, who had slept at the barn, was awake and loading suitcases into the back of the truck. He saw Doc's truck pull in and waved a greeting. As Doc parked the truck beside the barn, Meg decided to get something off her chest.

"Yesterday Tuck told me I couldn't have a real job with horses because I'm a hormonal girl." As soon as the words came out of Meg's mouth, she felt like a big ole tattle tale. She could hear Doc suck in his breath as he turned off the truck's engine.

Doc paused, deliberating over his next words. "Meg, you are smart. And you're a hard worker. You can do anything you put your mind to. But–"

"But what?"

"I want to put it gentle."

"Put what gentle?" Meg felt the blood boiling up her neck to her face.

Doc was no better than Tuck, telling her that girls couldn't do diddly squat.

"Meg, honey."

"Don't honey me, Doc. Tell it to me straight. But what?"

Doc let out an exasperated sigh. He rubbed his forehead. "Meg," he stopped himself. "Why do I feel like this is a conversation for your Aunt Louise?"

Meg shot Doc a hard stare.

"You—and girls in general—aren't usually jockeys. That's all."

"Why? Because a bunch of guys don't think we're tough enough or what?"

Doc shook his head. "It's not that. It's…it's just that after a certain age, girls develop different…and…and…those developments usually add weight to girls…not that it is bad… those..er…developments…that's just nature…Mother Nature… but…er…it adds weight. For a race…for a racehorse." Now it was Doc's turn to flush red.

"My developments aren't a handicap."

Doc stammered, "No…no…nor should you ever think that way…"

Before Doc could sort out his words, Tuck stuck his face into the passenger side window of the truck. "Your developments," Tuck laughed, rounding his hands out over his chest, "have not quite developed yet."

"Shut up," Meg spat at Tuck. "Mind your own *developments*."

"You got plenty of time to decide what you want to do with your life. Both of you." Doc climbed down from the truck, unloading his medical bags. "Developments or not. Meg, grab your suitcase and give it to Tuck to load."

"Bout time you all got here," Tuck said as he took Meg's

suitcase. "I've been checking tire pressure and double checking our gear since 4am."

Doc shot Tuck an irritated look.

Frank walked from the barn, an unlit cigarette dangling from his lips and a cup of black coffee in his hands. "Morning," Frank said. "Are we all loaded?"

Tuck replied, "Yes, sir. All except the horse."

Frank checked his wristwatch. 5:50am. "Right on time."

"I'll go get Ruffian," Meg said.

In the barn, Ruffian was running her muzzle through the remaining grain in her bin. She made happy little rumbling sounds when she ate.

"Morning, girl," Meg whispered as she slid open the stall door.

Ruffian lifted her head from her breakfast and wiped her face on Meg's t-shirt.

Meg chuckled, "I can't stay neat and tidy around you for one minute." She stroked Ruffian's neck. "You ready to run? Going to Belmont for your big maiden race."

As if she understood Meg's language, Ruffian's ears flicked forward. Meg noticed a spark of fire in Ruffian's eyes. "Oh, I think you're more than ready." Meg led Ruffian out to the horse trailer. As they walked out, Meg imagined Ruffian going all the way, all the way to the greatest glory a Thoroughbred could accomplish, the Triple Crown. Ruffian winning her maiden race and then sweeping the Kentucky Derby, then the Preakness, and then the Belmont. Her Ruffian.

Frank took the lead rope from Meg and loaded Ruffian

onto the trailer, carefully clipping her into the stall, checking her ankle wraps. When he was satisfied that she was safe, he closed the loading ramp and locked the door. "We got a long ride today. Fifteen, sixteen hours until Belmont. Doc, if we get separated along the way, we'll meet up at our planned watering stops."

"Got it," Doc confirmed. "Jacinto already gone?"

"Yep, he had to head out. Got a few other horses to ride before our race." Frank turned to Tuck, "Ready, young man? You can be my co-pilot." Tuck's chest puffed up like a male gorilla. Just as he had at school around all the girls. Meg was so mad she wanted to kick him. Tuck truly thought he was Frank's right hand man. "As if," Meg muttered.

"Meg, you ride with me. We got medical notes to talk about." Doc put his arm around her shoulders. She felt mildly better, almost appreciated.

Frank eased his truck and horse trailer out of the driveway and onto the highway. Doc followed in his pick-up. The sun shone gold and orange through the pine trees. Doc turned on the country western radio station and Meg gazed out the passenger's side window. Daydreaming. About Ruffian. Ruffian floating to the finish line without a competitor in sight, the crowds screaming out her name. She imagined all of the news reporters and headlines after the event, giving the world their first look at Ruffian. This Pegasus without wings. Her mind wandered to Belmont. She had never been to New York. When Doc told her mom and dad the week before, for once they seemed pleased with Meg, leaving her dumbstruck at the change in her parents.

It was odd, when she thought back on it. Her folks had driven over to Camden to pay them a surprise visit. They were sitting around Aunt Louise's kitchen table when Meg came home from school. Aunt Louise held Mom's hand. Mom glowed. Dad and Doc were on the back porch, smoking cigars. Her parents rushed to Meg and enveloped her in their arms.

"Look at you!" Mom said as she tried to twirl Meg around the kitchen.

Dad added, "You look like a real pro horse trainer. Dusty clothes and all."

Meg stuttered, "Th-thanks." She didn't think she looked any different than she did a few months ago.

"Meg is doing well here," Aunt Louise told them. "Real well. Her grades are up. She's playing the clarinet in the school band."

"That's nice," Mom smiled. "A change of scenery did you some good."

"Making friends?" Dad asked.

"A few," she admitted. "A couple of us head over to the Shake Stand and grab a burger and fries before I go to work at Frank's." Meg smiled as she thought about her friends Eliza and Sarah back in Kentucky. When she'd called them and told them about her after school job, Eliza had choked on her French Fries. "You mean training real racehorses? Ones that race?" Meg had laughed and teased Eliza, "Yeah, real racehorses, not fake ones that don't race." Sarah was just as amazed. "Isn't that dangerous?" she asked breathlessly. For once, Meg felt smart and strong and powerful. She felt that people—at least these two girls—admired her. That was a warm, spectacular sensation.

Mom clapped her hands and rattled Meg out of her daydream, "So glad you are fitting in!" Mom squealed again,

"Maybe you will go to prom." The way her mother purred the word *prom* pricked Meg like a shard of glass. *It always comes down to catching a boy,* Meg thought.

"What else you been doing?" Dad asked.

"I've been working with Mr. Whiteley, riding his horses. Grooming them, too."

Meg noticed her mother tense up just a smidge. She caught herself and her expression shifted to one of calm acceptance.

Dad said, "Guess you still love those ponies."

"Can't take that out of her. And who would want to?" Aunt Louise said.

Meg smiled, grateful that someone understood her. Yet she was uneasy. *Something was not quite right. But what?*

Her parents asked her about coming home at the end of the school year. It was Aunt Louise who came to her rescue. "Summer is our busy time at the barn. All kinds of vaccinations to give. We could sure use Meg's hands around here. Besides, Suzanne, you won't have any extra energy this summer if you're due in December." Aunt Louise paused and smiled placidly, "Get your rest. We'll look after Meg."

Mom heaved a resigned sigh and stroked her belly. Meg noticed a slight thickness to her mother's waist. Meg blinked her eyes and studied her physique again.

"Meg, sweetie," Mom cooed. "We're having a baby! Can you believe it?"

Meg's jaw dropped. *A baby.*

A baby.

A brother or a sister. Wasn't Mom too old to have a baby? She's

131

about what, forty? What the? I'm going to be a big sister. What in the world....

Mom said faintly, "If she's happy here and you don't mind having her..."

"We don't mind at all," Aunt Louise said.

"It would give me time to get the nursery all set up and the decorating all done..." her mother's eyes had a faraway look to them, one that reminded Meg of Rapunzel's eyes gazing from her tower as she dreams of finding her true love.

"It's settled then," Aunt Louise said, "Meg can stay with us through the summer."

Meg jumped up to hug Mom. "Thank you," she said. And she meant it.

Although Meg was relieved to be allowed to stay with Doc and Aunt Louise, the news of the pregnancy rattled her. Mom was no spring chicken. What would it be like to have a brother or sister who was sixteen years younger than her? It would be like raising two different families. Meg couldn't fathom it. *I won't have anything in common with this kid,* she thought, and then she felt relief. An odd sense of lightness. A baby would keep her mother busy and out of her hair. Meg prayed she'd just be allowed to stay with Aunt Louise until she graduated high school. That way she wouldn't even have to deal with the baby or her parents. They could spend all of their energy molding this new child. Just the way they want.

When Doc mentioned to her parents that he was taking Meg to Belmont, Dad argued, "She's too young to be around all that gambling and drinking. Good girls shouldn't see all that nonsense."

Doc reminded her father, "She won't be loitering around in the grandstand. She'll be working by my side. I'll let no one corrupt her."

Dad finally relented after Doc practically had to swear on a Bible to convince him that she'd be safe. Now, here they were, on the road to the races, Ruffian in the trailer ahead of them.

Doc glanced over at Meg. "Why so serious, kiddo?"

Meg, awoken out of her daydream, blinked. "Thinking about Mom and Dad. That's all."

Doc laughed, "Can you believe they let you go?"

"No. But they did. All thanks to you."

"Keep away from those track rats, like I promised them you would."

Meg grinned. "I won't fall for any sweet talking fella."

This time Doc chuckled, "I always knew you had brains."

The road to Belmont was slow. Traffic. Stops for water breaks. Road construction. They pulled into Belmont's barns after two in the morning. Frank, pepped up from drinking coffee all day and night, had a spring to his step. "We're here! Time to win a race, gorgeous," he sang to Ruffian as he led her off the trailer.

Doc examined Ruffian's legs for any sign of soreness or swelling. Trailers could do damage on a horse's legs. Everything looked and felt good. Still, Frank was never one to take risks. "Meg, ice her down in their wash racks. Twenty minutes on each leg. Then retire her for the night."

"Yes, sir." Meg iced all of Frank's horses. It was his go-to treatment plan for just about anything.

"Tuck, make sure she has plenty of soft bedding in her stall. We need her rested and fresh for her race."

Ruffian relaxed as Meg iced her legs. It was familiar. Routine. Comforting. Especially after a long day in a swaying trailer.

"There, there, girl. You feeling yourself? I bet you will after a good night's sleep." Meg took a towel and wiped the excess water off Ruffian's front legs.

Tuck, reclining in a lawn chair and snoring outside the stall, spooked when Ruffian swished her tail in his face as Meg led her inside. "She could've kicked me!" he whined.

"She could've but she didn't," Meg answered. "Cuz she's got class."

Meg settled Ruffian into her new stall.

"Where you sleeping?" Tuck asked.

"In the cot over there. Next to Doc's," she pointed to two camping cots in the corner of the barn. "Frank wants someone with her at all times."

"Lucky you. I'm hitching a ride to the hotel. See ya!" With that, Tuck sauntered from the barn.

She was feeling rather lucky. There was no place she'd rather be than right by her girl's side.

CHAPTER 19

The Maiden Race

May 22, 1974

They'd had four days to get Ruffian acclimated to Belmont. Meg had exercised Ruffian lightly on the track—until Jacinto got there. Then she had to let the professional take over. She didn't mind. She liked to watch Jacinto ride. He perched on a horse like a hummingbird, hovering in the wind.

Today was race day. Frank tried to keep a low profile, avoiding the press. He asked Tuck and Meg to stand guard by Ruffian's stall so no one could spook her or take photos of her. He wanted her right for her big maiden race, not all agitated because of people.

The maiden race was the third race of the day. It was a field of two-year-old fillies. They'd go just 5 ½ furlongs—five-eighths of a mile. The fillies would carry 116 pounds, no more, no less. To get down to racing weight, Jacinto and the other jockeys spent the morning in the sweat boxes, losing water weight from their bodies. Meg got the racing tack cleaned. She smoothed the cherry-red and white silks of Locust Hill Farm. Ruffian, with her deep midnight coat, would look stunning in the red silks.

"She ready?" Frank said, finishing yet another cup of coffee.

"Nearly, sir," Meg answered. She was working as quickly and as carefully as she could.

Mike Bell and Dan Williams, some of the grooms who also worked for Frank, came into the breezeway.

"Mr. Bell, would you please check my work?" Meg wanted to take no chances. She wanted every strap securely attached. Mike ran his hands over Ruffian's face, tugging at the bridle, checking the keepers on the headstall to make sure the leather was strong and fastened tight. His hands traveled down Ruffian's withers to her sides. Mike examined the saddle, then the girth. "Good job, kid. You've learned a lot since we first hired you."

Dan said, "Yeah, boss. She learned from the best of them. From me."

"Thanks." Meg knew Dan was top notch and that Mike was one of the best up-and-coming horsemen in the United States. It was an honor to receive praise from real pros.

Doc was up next. He checked Ruffian's legs, her leg wraps, he measured her breathing, her pulse. "Looking sound, Frank."

Frank pushed his hat back from his forehead. He scratched at his receding hairline. "Where's Jacinto?"

Jacinto, with a sparkle in his eyes, strode up to the team. "Is this gal ready to run? Cuz I sure am."

Frank came close to Jacinto's face. "Don't whip her hard. Let's see what she does on her own."

Jacinto, still smiling, said, "Frank, I got this, gringo. This chica is no problemo."

A bell rang out across the paddock. "Race three. Maiden race. Riders up," a voice announced from the loudspeaker. Goosebumps raced across Meg's arms. She felt the energy crackle in the air.

With a lift from Frank, Jacinto sprang into the saddle. Ruffian danced forward. Her eyes, like Jacinto's, sparkled. She arched her neck forward eagerly. She pranced through the crowds as Mike led them to the track. Doc, Tuck, and Meg crowded around the rail to watch the race. Frank had to hustle off to sit with the Janneys in the owner's box seats.

"Good luck," Meg shouted as she waved to Ruffian and Jacinto. "Show these folks who you are, girl. Show 'em what you got." This maiden race could set Ruffian on the path to greatness or to ruin. Meg prayed for greatness.

"Godspeed," Doc added. It sounded to Meg like a prayer.

Before Meg realized it, the fillies were loading into the starting gate. Hooves pounded against the metal in nervous anticipation. Jockeys shouted at the fillies, yelling orders at the young, spooked horses. Horses screamed in fright.

The starting bell rang. Ten fillies bounded from the gate. Suzest, the favorite, sprang off from the herd. Meg barely blinked and a big black filly barreled down on Suzest, overtaking her in a sheer second. Dirt flew across the track, up and across the equine bodies, coating the horses behind the leader—big, black, beautiful Ruffian. It was all Ruffian. Suzest struggled to stay with Ruffian, lunging and heaving to keep up. Meg watched as Ruffian's massive body hammered down the track. Suzest was falling, what looked like, miles behind Ruffian. Jacinto bobbed up and down with each stride. He didn't raise his whip, yet faster and faster Ruffian flew. With the wind, she sailed under the finish line. One minute, three seconds. Ruffian equaled the track record time! Suzest trailed behind her, finishing 15 lengths, 15 humiliating lengths, behind Ruffian—and placing second! Ruffian devoured her competition.

Meg, Doc, and Tuck grabbed each other, screaming, jumping at Ruffian's win. The crowd roared in excitement. The favorite, Suzest, had been bested. Ruffian! Ruffian was the two-year-old to watch.

In the winner's circle, Ruffian claimed her victory. She turned her elegant face toward Frank and Jacinto and then to the reporters for photographs, posing like a goddess in a painting.

"Vasquez! Vasquez!" a news reporter shouted at Jacinto. "Care to make a comment about that ride of yours?"

Jacinto smiled slyly, proud of their filly, "Ruffian sets her own pace and gets there on her own."

Ruffian twitched her ears in delight. *PFFFPPFFF!* She shot a stream of hot breath at the men, as if poking fun at them.

• • • • •

Back at the barn, Frank told his team, "Get yerself all scrubbed and purty." He clapped his hands, "You're going out on the town to celebrate."

Jacinto slapped Frank on the back, in triumph, "You gonna buy me dinner, boss man?"

"Oh heck no! You're going to make the rounds and smile for the cameras. Show America who the team to beat is."

Meg, finishing the tack cleaning, went over to her cot to rest.

"Young lady, that means you too," Frank said. "Go out and enjoy yourself for a change. I'll hold down the fort."

"You heard the man," Jacinto said, "Wash up and get your party clothes on!"

"Me, too?"

"Heck, yeah, gal. You, too. Shake a leg," Frank said.

Meg grabbed her suitcase from under the cot. Frank tossed a hotel room key to her. "Share that with your uncle. Be to dinner at eight." Frank leaned back in the cot and crossed his legs. He pulled his hat over his face, "Have fun and good night," he yawned.

When Jacinto took Meg on his arm and led her through the restaurant entrance, all eyes were on them. The crowd burst out in applause. Jacinto bowed. He winked at the pretty high society ladies—all of whom smiled and gave him dainty waves. He was obviously a favorite with the ladies. Doc and Tuck, wearing their pressed suits, shook hands with the other trainers and owners, accepting their congratulations. Meg, feeling self-conscious in her aunt's fire engine red dress, wanted to find a dark corner and just hide for the evening. The dress, she thought, was too clingy and too, well, too bright. She wished she could wear her jeans and a baggy t-shirt.

Three bird-like men flocked around Jacinto and Meg, speaking in Spanish. Meg caught bits and pieces of their animated conversation. They were jockeys, all of them had ridden earlier races in the day. All winners. And all ready to celebrate with Jacinto.

The jockey in the navy blue suit looked Meg up and down. He smiled like a hawk. "Que pasa, linda?" he asked Meg with an odd glimmer in his eyes. Meg shifted uncomfortably on her feet. The man looked ready to grab her in his talons.

Jacinto, finishing his conversation with another jockey, saw the interaction. He stepped between Meg and the jock. "Ah, easy boy, this lady is with me. Don't you be playing Romeo with her."

"With you? No way. You usually like them tall blondes. Let me talk to this pretty lady."

Meg turned as crimson as her dress. She had a guy trying to flirt with her and she didn't even realize it until Jacinto stepped in to ward him off. *I'm a real dolt,* she thought. *Truly.*

"Doc! Doc!" Jacinto sang out as he waved across the room. Doc saw him and weaved his way through the crowd, to the bar with Jacinto, Meg, and the flirty jockey. "Doc, tell Ramirez here, to leave this lady alone. Go on, you tell him she's with me. He don't believe me."

Doc lifted his drink in the air, "With you?" He shook his head. "No way. Don't fall for it, Ramirez. This gal is with me."

As if the situation couldn't get any more awkward, Tuck sprang into the gathering, slinging his arm around Meg's shoulders. "Actually, gentlemen, she's with me."

And that's when Meg had enough. She threw the rest of her Shirley Temple onto Tuck's suit jacket and stormed outside. *Like a piece of meat,* she thought. *Who do they think they are?*

The night air was warm and thick. But outside she could breathe. *Track rats.* Now she knew exactly what they had warned her about. She tugged at the hem of the red dress. It kept creeping up above her knees. As she sat at a patio table, Tuck flew from the restaurant, "Meg!" he called out.

"What?" she snapped.

"Why did you go and dump your drink on me? You stained

my new suit."

"I don't need you trying to protect me. Of all people."

"What the?"

"I was just fine."

"Oh, sure you were. *Sure.* That's why Jacinto and Doc circled you like a little lost lamb."

"I am not a lost lamb."

Meg took off her shoes. She rubbed her sore feet. She didn't feel like arguing with Tuck. What did he know anyway?

Tuck looked her in her eyes. "It is not meant as an insult, you know."

She rubbed her face in her hands. "What's not an insult? Having you act like my father or something?"

"Meg," Tuck paused, "We don't want these playboys chasing you. They like to party and they get rowdy real quick."

"So?"

"So, Doc and Jacinto—and me too—we didn't want anybody trying anything with you. Being disrespectful. You know?" It was Tuck who had his face in his hands now. "Geez, Meg, can you give me a break for once? I was trying to help you out."

Meg slugged Tuck in the shoulder.

"Ouch!"

"I could've done that if Ramirez had gotten too fresh with me."

Tuck rubbed his sore shoulder. "You could've just told me, not shown me."

"Sometimes showing is more effective." Meg smirked at Tuck.

It was Tuck who looked like a little lost lamb, in his crumpled suit with a bright red stain from a Shirley Temple down the front. There he sat, rubbing his tender shoulder. *Lost lamb, how does it feel?*

"We need a truce, Meg. Please."

"Why?"

"Cuz we're working for the same team and we're family." He straightened his necktie. "We need to act like grownups."

"That's real mature, coming from you, Tuck. Mister 'I'm gonna trash talk girls every chance I get.'"

"You looked real pretty in that dress tonight."

It had kind of felt nice to be thought of as pretty for a change. But she wasn't going to be taken advantage of or treated like a piece of meat. "Shut up," she said and walked back into the party. She was going to help herself to the buffet, find a nice seat by the piano, and enjoy her dinner in peace. If a guy tried to get fresh with her, she planned to handle it all by herself, maybe not with her fists per se, but she could hold her own—she realized that now. She'd lift her head like Ruffian does, swish her metaphorical tail, and snort at the fellas. She didn't have time for their games. *Man,* she thought, glancing at her wristwatch, *when can I head back to the barn?*

CHAPTER 20

The Fashion Stakes

June 12, 1974

Belmont, New York

Frank hadn't let the team celebrate much after Ruffian's first win. Just one night of fun. "Could be beginner's luck," he reminded them.

"Ah, Frank, I know luck when I feel it," Jacinto said, "She has something else. She has IT."

"It what?" asked Meg.

"She is fierce. And fast. She is world-class," Jacinto paused. "She's the fastest filly I've ever seen. The girl's got swagger."

"She knows it. Doesn't she? She knows she's a champion fighter," Meg added.

"Yeah, she's a champ alright. These horses, they don't all have it."

"You better not tell too many people that. We don't want word spreading among the bookies," Frank snapped at them. "We got a race to focus on today. Jacinto, get your tail to the sweat box and make weight."

"Yeah, yeah, Frank. But if I win this afternoon, you are buying me a big, fat, juicy steak for dinner."

"Arrogant jocks," Frank muttered as Jacinto walked away. Meg smirked but tried to hide it. She liked to watch Jacinto fool around with Frank. Frank was all business. Jacinto was all play— until he was on the back of a horse. Then he was business, too. *Man,* she thought, *these guys are the best in the business. And I get to work with them. Talk about a streak of luck.*

Meg hustled into Ruffian's stall. She picked Ruffian's hooves clean. Ruffian seemed jumpier today, as if her first victory a couple weeks ago had given her a taste of something sweet and she eagerly wanted more. "Whoa, girl. Stop your wiggling," Meg said as she dug out the last bit of dirt from around Ruffian's frog on her front right hoof.

Mike stuck his head into the stall. Ruffian snorted at him. "What's got into her?"

"She's as impatient as all get-out."

"Tell her to save her energy for the race. We don't need no diva in the paddock," Mike said. He grabbed Ruffian's nose and tugged at it playfully. She snorted again.

Tuck came running. "Frank says five minutes to riders up." He had two large bags of ice in his arms.

"Stick 'em in the cooler," Mike instructed him, pointing to the tack room next to Ruffian's stall. "We'll need 'em after the race."

Unloading the ice bags, Tuck asked, "Has Doc checked her over?"

Mike shook his head. "He's checking over a horse from the last race."

"I hope he gets here quick," Meg said, "before we have to go out."

Doc, with a stethoscope around his neck, came jogging toward them, "Hey! You ready?"

"Just waiting on you," Mike said, relieved Doc made it on time.

Doc examined Ruffian, checking her vitals. "All clear," he said and patted her on the rump. "Go get 'em, big girl."

Meg stood on her tiptoes and planted a kiss right on Ruffian's nose. "A kiss for good luck," she whispered to Ruffian. Ruffian snorted again and pulled her head away.

"Looks like she doesn't want to be babied before a race," Mike joked as he led Ruffian to the paddock to join Jacinto.

As Meg sidled up to the race track rail, she wondered how Ruffian would do this afternoon, her second race. It was the same length as her first, 5 ½ furlongs. Six fillies on the field, each carrying 117 pounds. Frank had said her biggest threat would be Copernica, a bay filly who was born blind in her left eye. Blind but tough, Jacinto had told Meg. "Don't you ever underestimate a horse or a person," Jacinto reminded her. He then winked at her, "We'll take her though." Ruffian, Meg knew, could handle any competitor. How fast would Jacinto let Ruffian go? Would he let her go all out? Or would he hold her back and let Ruffian feel the maddening chase of the herd?

Meg heard the starting bell sound.

The horses were off!

Jacinto and Ruffian were stuck in the middle of the pack. Horses jostled for position. Jan Verzal took the early lead. Ruffian came out pumping, swerving for a position, securing second. *Second! How that must drive the filly mad,* Meg thought. They hit the half-mile mark. Meg noticed the slightest shift, like a race car shifting into higher gear. Ruffian plunged forward, a head at first. Ruffian! Ruffian takes the lead. Edging, edging away from the thundering herd. Going, going, going…sweeping down the stretch. Meg swore she could see wings sprout from Ruffian as she soared past the grandstand. A win! One minute and three seconds flat.

Cheering madly, Meg screamed Ruffian's name. Her girl! Two for two!

On the far side of the track, Jacinto brought Ruffian down to a walk. Her ears twitched at the avalanche of applause. Jacinto, glorious in the red and white silks, stroked Ruffian's neck. Reporters swarmed them in the winner's circle. Meg and Tuck were pushed aside as the reporters jostled for Jacinto, Frank, and the Janneys. Tuck smiled at Meg, "Looks like we're chopped liver…you should've wore your red dress."

Meg tossed her head in the air, "Did you get the Shirley Temple out of your suit?"

Tuck laughed it off. "Whoa, girl! Be nice," he sang to Meg. "Truce. Remember?"

Meg, feeling like a champion herself, stood next to Tuck, smiling at Ruffian and their team.

"Mr. Whiteley, congratulations," a reporter said, "Ruffian set a track record today—and this race has been run since 1897. Quite an accomplishment." The reporter reached out to shake Frank's hand.

"Thank you," Frank, never chatty with reporters, replied.

The reporter looked up at Jacinto, still mounted on Ruffian.

"You left Copernica six-and-three-quarters lengths back. How did you do it?"

"I didn't do nothing. I just sit on the horse. She did all the work. Ask her," Jacinto answered. Ruffian reached out and nipped at the reporter. "She's always hungry after a race," Jacinto joked. More cameras flashed in Ruffian's face.

Jacinto told the reporters, "It's like she's playing a game out there on the course. And she's the one making up the rules. And the one who is winning." It was obvious he loved Ruffian's tough girl charm, her smarts, and her talent. After today, so would all of America.

Here, at Belmont, Ruffian had made a name for herself. Here she wouldn't be forgotten. Meg repeated Jacinto's words to herself, "It's like she's playing a game out there on the course. And she's the one making up the rules. And the one who is winning." Meg decided those were wise words to live by.

CHAPTER 21

The Summer of 1974

Careful to let her rest from her two big wins, Frank had Meg and Mike give Ruffian light workouts and ice after each one. Meg had been assigned other horses to work with—in addition to caring for Ruffian. She'd had the chance to exercise a few two-year-olds all because she'd been bold. One afternoon, she'd been helping Frank lead a string of two-year-old colts out to the practice track. One of the exercise jockeys took a tumble. He'd only suffered a broken collar bone but Frank, frustrated by the setback, kicked and cussed at the dirt as the jockey hobbled off the track. Meg wasted no time. She sprung on the next colt's back, secured her helmet, and cantered off—all before Frank could say a word. Since then, she was a groom and exercise jockey to boot.

By early July, Frank had news for the crew.

"We're hauling Ruffian to Aqueduct. She'll run the Astoria Stakes," Frank informed them as they sat around a table at Mel's Diner, feasting on bacon and eggs, and, of course, coffee.

Mike scribbled notes in his binder. "Who's she running against?"

"Laughing Bridge. Jan Verzal."

Mike rubbed his eyes, exhausted from long work days, "Strong field of fillies."

Meg finished chewing her bacon and spoke up, "Jan Verzal gave her a good run in the last race. She placed third, I think."

Frank nodded, "Yep, this race will surely prove what Ruffian has got." Frank drummed his fingers on the table. "We've got to change things up some for this race."

Mike asked, "What for, Frank? Things are going good."

"Jacinto ain't gonna ride."

"Why not?" asked Meg. She liked hanging around Jacinto, hearing about his escapades at the tracks.

"Seems that Mr. Vasquez got himself a ten-day penalty due to bumping into someone's horse in another race. That's why." Frank did not look pleased.

Without missing a beat, Mike asked, "Who you got lined up, boss?"

"Vince Bracciale. He's solid. Dependable." Frank motioned for the bill. "We just keep up our part of the deal. Give him a sound horse to ride."

● ● ● ● ●

At Aqueduct Racetrack, for the Astoria Stakes, Ruffian high stepped into the paddock. Meg held her reins while Mike hoisted Vince Bracciale into the saddle. "She moves. Don't let her get away with you," Mike advised Vince as he checked Ruffian's girth strap yet again.

"I think I can handle a filly, no matter how big she is," Vince said as he secured his helmet and goggles. "Let's roll." Vince took Ruffian out to the starting gate.

The fillies loaded into the gate. They were sweaty and tense. The anxious fillies screamed as they crammed into the boxes. The jockeys gathered the reins and manes in their hands, settling their bodies into position, checking their helmets and goggles. The bell rang out. The chutes sprung open. Ruffian broke from the pack early, seizing the lead. Laughing Bridge was lengths behind without a chance. *Where were the others?* Meg saw the other fillies running, jostling, struggling, fighting for the lead over one another, but it was no use. Ruffian was gone. Gone! Meg saw that Vince never looked over his shoulder, never looked behind him. Not once. It was as if Ruffian was the only horse in the race. All Ruffian. Ruffian glided across the finish line. No competition.

Back at Ruffian's stall, Meg began her routine. Bathe Ruffian, then ice each leg. Mike supervised her, making sure she never took a short cut. Ruffian shivered when the cool water hit her skin. "You did good, girl," Meg praised Ruffian. Vince, changed into his street clothes, stopped by the barn. "Frank around?" he asked Meg, who pointed to the tack room. "Talking to the Janneys," she told him.

"Keep up the good work, kid, with that horse. You'll go far."

"Thank you, Mr. Bracciale. Did you like her?"

"Like her? She's terrific. A real cruiser."

By the time Meg finished with Ruffian, Vince was long gone. Mike and Frank huddled near the phone in the tack room.

She could hear Frank speak into the receiver, "We got a little over two weeks. Yes, ma'am. She'll be ready. Jacinto will be back. I'll be sure to book him."

Mike noticed Meg peaking around the corner. "Hey, Meg!

We're going to the Jersey Shore. To Monmouth!"

"Jersey!" Meg was getting to see the whole world, it felt like. She wasn't cooped up with her parents in the safe, bland old suburbs. She was an honest-to-goodness professional, traveling the world, winning races, meeting famous jockeys and trainers. She was doing things. *Take that, suburbia,* she thought.

Frank, finishing his phone conversation, turned to them. "A longer race and a bigger purse. Can you two handle it?"

Meg delighted, replied, "Yes, sir!" She and Ruffian could conquer the world. Her big, beautiful filly was unbeatable. Ruffian, the gladiator!

"Good, I'll go tell Tuck and Doc. We got some work to do!"

"Don't we always have work to do?" Meg asked Mike.

"Don't you know it, kid," Mike said.

● ● ● ● ●

"July 27, 1974, the 19th running of the Sorority Stakes. A six furlong course for the nation's best two-year-old fillies," the television newscaster spoke into the microphone. Frank stood uneasily in front of Ruffian's stall, waiting for his interview. "Does the unbeaten Ruffian, the big black beauty from the South, have what it takes?"

Frank cleared his throat, choosing his words carefully, "Ruffian is getting stronger with each race. Each race she taps into another gear we didn't know she had. But everyone in the horse business knows that anything can happen. We'll just hope fortune is on her side again today."

"Thank you, Mr. Whiteley," the newscaster concluded, happy with the sound bite Frank had given him. "And now to the starting line." The camera crew scurried away. Meg popped out from behind Frank. She had been crouching in the stall, holding Ruffian by a lead rope so she wouldn't lash out and chomp down on a cameraman.

"Yes, you can come out now," Frank smiled at her.

Ruffian shifted on her feet, shaking her head at Frank.

Frank looked Ruffian in the eyes, "I'll let you taste them next time. Promise."

Meg enjoyed Frank's wry sense of humor even though he didn't let it show often. "I'm gonna hold you to that, sir."

"Vas-QUEZ!" Frank called through the barn, "Where the heck are you, man!"

Jacinto and Mike hustled toward Frank. They'd finished weigh-in and it was riders up. With a cat-like bounce, Jacinto was on Ruffian. "I'm back, chica!" he smiled as he stroked her neck. Ruffian huffed, lifted her tail and left the crew a large, warm pile of manure.

"Ya-Ha! Now she's ready to run!" Jacinto laughed.

Taking her usual position at the rail with Doc and Tuck, Meg admired Ruffian as she strutted toward the starting gate. Ruffian arched her neck, lifting her feet high in the air.

"She's regal," Meg said quietly to them.

"Ain't she?" Tuck agreed. "I never really thought much about fillies until her."

"Isn't that how you feel about girls, in general?"

"What's that supposed to mean?"

"You know what I mean. You think girls aren't as good just like you think fillies aren't as good as colts."

Embarrassed to be called out by Meg, he grumbled out a "Nuh-uh."

"I don't see many fillies built like her," Doc said, distracting Meg and Tuck from their nitpicking, "She's massive, yet delicate. And that fierceness in her eyes. She's a fighter."

The four fillies loaded into the starting gate and, with a roar, the gates sprung open, and the crowds unleashed their mighty yells.

From the get-go, Ruffian was neck and neck with Hot N Nasty, a big, undefeated filly. Ruffian edged her nose ahead. Hot N Nasty crept up. Back and forth, back and forth, stride for stride, until the quarter mile. At the homestretch, Hot N Nasty on the outside, Ruffian on the rail. The finish line was coming and Hot N Nasty couldn't be shaken.

Would she beat Ruffian? No horse had so far. "Go girl!" Meg shouted above the crowd, "GO!!!!!!!!!!" She might lose, the thought crossed Meg's mind. "NO!!!" Meg screamed. "RUN!!!"

Jacinto lifted his whip and brought it down on Ruffian. She reacted. She found her next gear and pushed forward, taking the lead. She ran with all her heart, never relenting, refusing to be beaten. She roared toward the finish line, winning by two-and-a-quarter lengths.

"Ohmygod!" Meg cried into Doc's arms, "I didn't know if she could do it!"

Tuck, jumping and punching his fists in the air, shouted, "Take that, Hot N Nasty! Now you're defeated!"

"You've had a change of tune, haven't you?" Meg asked Tuck.

"Hey, we're one team here," Doc scolded them. "Remember that, one team with a common goal." Doc reached for his medical bag. "Come on, she might be spent. Let's get down there and give Mike and Jacinto a hand."

The Janneys and Frank were in the Winner's Circle, accepting the purse prize—over $62,000—and their trophy. Meg had never heard of so much money in her life—yet here it was, earned in less than five minutes. Jacinto, dismounting, grinning like a cat who just ate a prized canary, told reporters, "She moves like a Cadillac when you ask for more gas."

• • • • •

Rest was critical for a racehorse. Push them too much, too soon, too hard and injury would surely follow. Frank took rest and rehab seriously. They'd had almost a month off and Ruffian was fit to be tied. Meg had spent the month working with Mike as he prepped the other two-year-olds for sale. Meg, like Ruffian, was eager to get back to the races. She walked Ruffian through the dim breezeway, gently warming her up before post time. The horse sensed it was showtime. Her muscles twitched. She spooked at every new sound or person. Frank hoped walking her out would put her in the right frame of mind. Meg had been walking her for an hour.

"Bring her back in," Frank instructed as he approached them. "Time for her race."

Ruffian whinnied at the word "race."

As Meg and Mike readied Ruffian, she couldn't stand still.

"I thought you walked her?" Mike snapped at her.

Meg, her arms aching from holding tightly to a twitchy, thousand-pound filly, barked back, "I did and she's still feisty."

"Jeezus, she's worse than a colt, getting all worked up."

"What's the weight today?" She asked as she clipped Ruffian to the stall.

"120 on all of 'em."

"Six furlongs with Vince on board?"

"Yes, ma'am."

The increased distance worried Meg—three-quarters of a mile—but more so over the increased weight on her back. One hundred and twenty pounds—the most she's ever had.

"Don't look so grim, kid. This is Saratoga. The Spa. Millionaire's Playground. Party central." Mike grunted as he cinched Ruffian's saddle. She blew out and kicked at him with her hind leg.

"I wish Jacinto was riding her. He gets her buttons," Meg said.

"Me, too. But he landed another suspension. That rascal. Maybe we'll get him for the next race."

Mike mussed up Meg's ponytail. "I could put you on her and she'd win," he joked.

"Doubtful. I don't make weight," Meg pointed out. She half chuckled to herself, remembering Doc's awkward conversation with her months ago about girls and their *er, developments*. She was getting her *developments* and then some.

Mike patted his belly, "Me neither. Me neither."

"Post time," Tuck called as he ran toward them. "Riders up!"

They led Ruffian to the paddock where Vince was ready and waiting. "I'll see you folks in the winner's circle," Vince said when he was seated on Ruffian's back.

One minute and eight seconds after the gates sprung open, Ruffian won the Spinaway Stakes, leaving Laughing Bridge thirteen lengths in her wake. Thirteen lengths! Not a race at all—it was carnage. Ruffian blew past the finish line. *Gladiator,* Meg thought as she watched Vince bring Ruffian down to a trot at the far turn.

In the winner's circle after the race, Meg held Ruffian's reins and looked on as Vince handled the reporters' questions.

"You plan on being her permanent rider?"

Vince smiled modestly, "That's not up to me. That's up to Mr. Whiteley. I just do what I'm told."

"Did you know how fast she was moving?"

Vince answered, "A minute eleven…I never really let her run, you know."

The reporter spoke up, "You ran 1.083. A Spinaway record. AND," the reporter added dramatically, "a record time for any two-year-old at this distance at Saratoga."

Another reported chimed in, "They've been racing here since the Civil War!"

"You think she can go faster?" another reporter asked. Meg knew Ruffian could go faster. She knew Ruffian would give all it takes to win—no matter what.

Vince shrugged, "You saw me. I was pulling her up, trying to slow her all the way home." Vince thought for a moment, "I think only Ruffian knows what she's got."

Cameras flashed in their faces. Ruffian eager to get back to her stall to eat, neighed across the winner's circle. Vince hopped down, "Here you go, kid."

Meg led the dancing filly back to the barn.

CHAPTER 22

Off

After winning the Spinaway Stakes, something about Ruffian seemed off-kilter.

"Her eyes don't look right," Meg told Mike.

"You mean she don't look like the devil," Mike said as he measured out grain for the other horses.

"I can't put my finger on it," Meg puzzled. "She's off."

"I'll take a look and if something seems wrong, I'll get Frank." Mike pulled the grain cart down the alleyway as hungry horses nickered for him. "No worries, kid. We all got that horse's best interest at heart. She's the Queen Bee."

Later that morning, after all the horses had been fed and watered, Mike and Meg found Frank and brought him to Ruffian's stall. "Ruffian's not eaten breakfast and she's running a fever, Frank." Mike said.

Frank bent down and examined Ruffian's legs, checking for any sign of lameness.

"Easy, girl," he said to Ruffian, "Why would a strong girl like you skip breakfast?"

Ruffian bent and nuzzled her head into Frank. He scratched her between her ears. "Get Doc. Something's off with her. She's not being her feisty self. She's acting like a lapdog."

Always thorough in his examinations, Doc ran his hands over Ruffian's long legs. "Horses can tweak themselves. Get sore muscles. Hard to spot sometimes," Doc said to Meg as he continued examining Ruffian. "Let's take a few x-rays."

Ruffian, feverish and listless, lowered her head to nestle into Meg's chest. "Oh, girl, Doc is going to see what's wrong and make you all better. Just wait and see. Right, Doc?" Meg was getting more worried as Ruffian nestled deeper into her. She wasn't playful. She wasn't sassy. Ruffian seemed listless, exhausted. Her deep brown eyes, usually sparkling in mischief, were dull as stones.

"I always try my best," Doc said.

After the x-rays, Doc reported back to Frank and the team. "I found a hairline fracture in Ruffian's right hind pastern."

"And?" Frank asked.

"Frank, she has Native Dancer blood running through her veins. He was known for speed and fragility. We've got to watch her bones. They're brittle as bird bones."

Meg knew Ruffian's lineage better than her own family tree. She had speed in her bloodlines but also one tragic, fatal flaw— her Achilles heel, these brittle bones. Meg rarely witnessed her uncle so tentative, hesitant.

Doc went on, "She's done for as a two-year-old. She needs rest. Time to recover. She might come back as a three-year-old. If we are careful."

Meg felt her heart sink to her feet. *Done for. Might come back. If we are careful. If, if, if, the worst word in the English language, if.* That's all she heard. Her brain felt foggy, clouded, buried with the if.

Frank said, "I try to be hopeful but I am a realist. Any sort of fracture could signal the end of a racehorse's career."

"Precisely," Doc responded. "Only time will tell how she heals. We're going to put her in a soft jelly cast. We'll change it every 48 hours and x-ray her again in thirty days. If she shows improvement…"

If.

CHAPTER 23

Rest

Frank's team looked after Ruffian around the clock. Since Doc's diagnosis, she'd been confined to her stall and had her legs iced three times a day. Meg handled the late afternoon icing, along with feeding her. *If* echoed through Meg's brain as she tended to the horse.

The *if* in Meg's brain had subsided ever so slightly when Ruffian's fever broke. Doc said it was a promising sign but reminded them that she "wasn't out of the woods yet."

Meg measured out Ruffian's grain and filled her water buckets with fresh water. "There you are. All set for dinner." Ruffian nickered in quiet pleasure.

"Meg!" Doc shouted through the barn. "Come to the office when you're done with her."

Meg never kept Doc waiting. She rubbed Ruffian's neck real quick and jogged down to meet Doc in the office.

Doc sat at the desk. "Take a seat."

She thought she was in serious trouble. Had she forgotten to do something or put away the tack?

Without giving her a chance to speak, Doc said, "I've been on the phone with your parents." He drummed his fingers on the desk, choosing his words. "Your mother is on bed rest."

"I don't understand. Why?"

"She's had some complications with the pregnancy. Her doctor wants her to take it easy for a couple more weeks. To see if the baby makes it to term." Doc watched Meg to gauge her reaction. "We think you should head back to Kentucky. Spend time with your mother. Help her out some."

Meg didn't particularly want to go back to Kentucky. She didn't want to be stuck with her mother, listening to her criticize her horse friends and her lack of boyfriends. She belonged here, at the barn, with her people, most of all, with her horse. Meg pleaded, "But, what about, what about Ruffian? Who's going to look after her?"

Doc came around from the desk and sat on the edge of it. "Meg, Frank has the best team in the business. Don't you worry one bit. Frank, Mike, and Barclay can manage Ruffian. They've got other grooms, too, like Minnor, who can tend to her. She'll be okay."

"I…I…I don't want to leave her," Meg tried to fight back tears. Ruffian was her girl. Her girl.

Doc took Meg's hands in his, "Meg, your mom needs you. If she loses this baby, she'll be devastated. Go. Go help her. I won't let anything bad happen to Ruffian. We'll get her on the mend. Aunt Louise will drive you back to Kentucky."

• • • • •

Meg entered her parents' home. The house, normally spotless, had a look of dishevelment. Meg noted the dust on the bookshelves and the stack of dirty dishes in the kitchen sink.

"Your mother is upstairs. In her bedroom," Aunt Louise told her as she set the suitcase in the family room. "Go let her know you're here while I freshen up."

Meg climbed up the stairs, swallowing hard. Everything looked familiar yet strange as if she'd been gone a lifetime. She'd never seen her mother truly sick before. What would she look like? Pale? Boney? Bloodless? She shivered as she turned the door knob on the bedroom door.

She stepped into the dim bedroom.

Mom sighed, sitting up in her bed. "My girl. Give me a hug. I've missed you."

She leaned into her mother's arms. Meg thought Mom looked tired, pale, worried. She noticed the stack of magazines on the nightstand.

"Bed rest is not my style," Mom said. "I'm practically bored out of my mind. The house is probably a disaster—your father is not much of a housekeeper. How many back issues of *Life* magazine can a woman read?" Mom half laughed. "Meg, honey, are you okay?"

Meg shook her head yes then no.

"Baby, what's the matter?"

And that's when Meg let the tears flow. In deep, gulping sobs she told her mother all about Ruffian, her races, and her injury. "She might not race again," she sobbed. Mom stroked her hair and listened.

As her sobs slowed, Mom whispered into Meg's ear, "Oh baby, I had no idea. I am so, so sorry." She paused, "This horse means that much to you."

Meg quieted in her mother's arms and answered, "She's my best friend."

•••••

Meg spent the next week tidying the house, doing laundry, cooking meals. She dropped dog-tired into bed each night. Her father, off at work all day, came home to eat dinner and read the evening newspaper. For once, Meg saw the full scope of her mother's work, of her life.

Bed rest meant exactly that. Mom was only allowed to get up and walk to the bathroom and shower. Nothing strenuous. No lifting. So Meg moved the television set upstairs. During the afternoons, they watched "The Phil Donahue Show" together. The weeks blurred by. All of the days were ordinary, in every ordinary way. Breakfast, lunch, TV hour, dinner. Dishes. *Rinse and repeat.* Meg wondered how Ruffian was recovering, what Tuck was doing…she missed the rhythms and smells of the barn, the horses. She missed the sunshine, the fresh air.

Late one afternoon, as Meg tried her darnedest to shape a slab of hamburger into meatloaf on a pan, she heard her mother unleash a blood-curdling screech. "MEGGGGG!"

She ran upstairs. "Mom!"

Mom, crouched on the bathroom floor, was panting and holding her belly.

"Dad," Meg stuttered, "Dad, I'll call Dad."

She shook her head. "No, not yet…oooo…huff…huff… shoo…oooo!"

"How close are the contractions?"

"I. Don't. Knooooooow," she moaned.

The contractions were coming on awfully hard and fast. There was no way that Dad would be able to drive all the way from his office to their house and take Mom all the way to the hospital. Not the way the contractions shook her body. No way.

She rushed downstairs to the telephone. Her hands trembling, she dialed 9-1-1. "Ambulance. 848 Wilson Drive. My mom is having a baby. Right now. HURRY! PLEASE!"

She slammed the phone back onto the receiver and ran back upstairs. Mom was groaning in the bathroom. "Pfff, pff, pff," she exhaled in cadence. A contraction rolled through her body again.

"Call. Your. Father. At work."

"He won't make it in time!"

"Call your father!"

Meg rushed downstairs to the kitchen again, fumbling in Mom's Rolodex for Dad's work number.

"Pff, Pff, pff," Lamaze breaths, came from the bathroom, louder and quicker this time. Meg didn't have time to talk on the phone. Mom was having a baby. She flew to the linen closet. Fresh towel. A bucket. No, a big bowl of water. What else had Doc used at the barn?

"MEGGGGGG!!!!!!"

"Coming!"

Loaded with clean towels, Meg knelt by her mother's side. "Breathe, breathe." Meg pushed down her panic. She tried to shut out her mother's screaming, to concentrate and remember Doc's lessons. *As with horses, it is with people.* She'd watched Doc deliver plenty of foals. *But foals…*Meg shuddered…*ohmygod ohmygod… breathe.*

Mom clenched her teeth. "Ohmygod, it's coming!"

"Attagirl. You got this," Meg told her, just like Doc did with the horses.

She wiped her mom's brow with a towel. "Easy, easy. Relax. Breathe."

Trying to settle into the rhythmic breathing, Mom moaned again, "OOOOO…ooooo…OOOOO!"

Meg saw a head crowning. That was a promising sign. Head first. Not a breech birth. "Come on, baby, easy does it."

Mom shrieked louder. Meg, gathering another clean towel, crouched down. "Wait, don't push, wait…" Meg waited for the contraction, "Push! Now! Push!"

In a wave of fluids, a red-faced baby wriggled out, almost getting stuck. Meg gently tugged the baby's torso to get its legs free. Then she held a red, angry-looking baby in her hands. She gingerly toweled the baby off, counting its fingers and toes. The baby let out an earth-moving wail. Mom's breathing slowed and steadied.

"Mom, it's a girl. A big strong girl."

Tears rolled down Mom's face as Meg placed the baby in her arms.

"She's perfect," Mom cooed to the baby. She looked to Meg. "Thank you, my Meggie."

The ambulance siren pierced their solitude. The EMTs rushed into the house and carried Mom and the baby away to the hospital.

Standing by her mother's hospital bed later that evening, Meg held her baby sister. Her sister. Her sister with the scrunched up, angry face, with the wisps of jet-black hair, and the teeny round toes. *She is adorable,* Meg thought, *completely adorable.* Dad snapped photographs with his Polaroid camera. "Look at my beautiful girls," he trumpeted. "My three gorgeous girls."

A nurse with a clipboard entered the room. "Congratulations, Mr. and Mrs. Murphy. And you, little miss, I heard you delivered your sister. My, oh my! You should go into medicine."

Meg smiled at the nurse and then at her sister.

"I got the birth certificate paperwork here for you all to fill out. What are you planning to name your new baby?" the nurse asked.

"Sophie Ann Murphy," Mom answered.

"Lovely, lovely choice for a name," the nurse said.

"I think so. It's after a very special horse."

A warm, cozy feeling wrapped itself around Meg. A feeling she hadn't allowed herself to feel for a very long time. Mom remembered Meg's story about giving Ruffian the name Sophie— because she was as soft and smooth as a sofa.

CHAPTER 24

Back in Camden

April 2, 1975

"Aren't you glad to be back?" Tuck asked Meg as he set her luggage on Aunt Louise's front porch in Camden.

Meg, tired from the bus ride, rubbed her eyes. "Don't get me wrong. My mom and dad are much more chill since Sophie came along. She keeps them hopping. But I missed you guys and Ruffian."

"Did Doc tell ya she's all healed and Frank's gonna run her?"

Meg couldn't contain her joy. "Yeah, as soon as Doc told me, I begged my mom to let me come back here."

"I can't believe she let you."

"Things are different between us. She's treating me more like a person, an adult—it's really kinda nice."

"Well, nothing has changed here. Frank is still Frank. And Mike, too. They've been letting me work with some of the new two-year-olds, riding them and working with Minnor and Barclay. It's a heck of a lot of fun. I'm glad my folks let me stay in South Carolina this year. A chance of a lifetime. That's what my pop said." He paused and let out a chuckle. "He doesn't even care that I actually live in the barn and sleep in the loft. As long as I go to school and get my tail to work." Meg was a bit envious of the freedom Tuck had as a guy. His parents didn't fuss or worry about him. He could do as he pleased. "He knows Doc always keeps me in line."

Meg found the house key under the welcome mat. She unlocked the front door. "Thanks for meeting me at the bus station, Tuck."

"Anytime."

"See you tomorrow." She leaned in to give him a quick hug.

"See ya, Meg."

Since everyone was at work, Meg went upstairs, crawled into the guest bed and fell asleep. She needed to get her rest. Tomorrow she'd report back to work at the barn.

•••••

Ruffian tossed her head in the air and whinnied when she saw Meg.

"Baby girl!" Meg said excitedly. She took Ruffian's muzzle in her hands and brought it to her lips. *Smmph.* "A kiss for you!" Meg laughed at the horse. Ruffian nickered and buried her head in Meg's chest as Meg scratched Ruffian's forehead. "Frank said I could take you out for a spin, a nice, light trot. Sound like fun to you?"

Eager to get back in the saddle, Meg tacked up Ruffian as quick as a flash of lightning. At the practice track, Meg climbed up. "Nice and easy, girl, nice and easy." Meg clicked her tongue to her teeth. Ruffian picked up the cue, one two, one two. Meg held her at a posting trot around the track even though she could feel Ruffian's desire to fly. The sunshine, the horse, the delicious spring air. The world was as perfect as it could ever get.

CHAPTER 25

To the Races

The Spring of 1975

"Have a great time. And good luck to your girl," Mom said over the telephone line. "I'll see you at graduation in June. Love you."

"Thanks, Mom. Give Sophie a kiss for me. And Dad, too. I love you."

Meg hung up the phone, ready to return to the road with Ruffian.

For the next two months, Ruffian ran.

April 14, 1975. Aqueduct. Six furlongs. Win. 1:08 3/5.

April 30, 1975. Aqueduct. Seven furlongs. Comely Stakes. Win. 1:20 1/5.

May 10, 1975. Aqueduct. 1 mile. Acorn Stakes. Win. 1:33 1/5.

May 31, 1975. Aqueduct. 1 1/8 miles. Mother Goose Stakes. Win. 1:47.

After the Mother Goose Stakes, Meg rushed back to Camden to graduate, fulfilling her promise to her parents. Three days later, she hit the road again to catch up with Ruffian in New York.

June 21, 1975. Belmont. 1 ½ miles. Coaching Club American Oaks. Win. 2:24.

The accolades piled on Ruffian and on Frank's team. She'd won the Triple Tiara, the Triple Crown for fillies. Newspaper reporters, television crews, fans, all wanted to get close to America's fastest filly. Other jockeys whispered about Ruffian. "It's like trying to catch a ghost," they said. Frank hired guards to keep people away from his barn. Meg, Tuck, and Mike kept their noses down and tended to Ruffian. "No interviews," Frank instructed them. "Keep your mind on the race ahead."

Meg knew when Frank worried. He always pushed his hat back and scratched at his balding head. Tonight he not only looked worried, he looked angry.

"They're putting her into a match race," Frank said as he flung himself into the lawn chair outside of Ruffian's stall.

Mike asked, "Against?"

"A colt of all things! The press and the racing association want a Girl Versus Boy match race. A real battle of the sexes." Frank's cheeks were red.

Trying to be optimistic, Meg said, "That could be fun. Ruffian can take any boy—and win!"

Frank didn't appreciate the comment. "That's beside the point. I don't believe in running fillies against colts. Never have. And match races are just plain trouble. Two horses, lots of noise and energy. Two horses that only want to win…nothing but trouble."

"Do we have to run her?" Mike asked.

"Yep, her owners committed to it. We've gotta do it."

"Well, since that's that, what are the details, Frank?" Mike took a small notepad and pen out of his jeans pocket.

"Belmont. July 6."

Mike scribbled down the details. "And her competitor?"

Frank, disgusted, replied, "Foolish Pleasure. The Kentucky Derby winner." A string of expletives flew from Frank's lips. "The colt outta Williston, Florida, not even a Kentucky-born horse."

Mike settled Frank down, "Boss man, get Jacinto on her. We'll show Foolish Pleasure and the world what this girl's got."

CHAPTER 26

Match Race

July 6, 1975

Meg saved all of the newspaper clippings about her girl. She tucked them away in her scrapbook. Her favorites were the photographs of Ruffian looking fierce and regal as she strode to the starting gate. She'd even clipped a snippet of Ruffian's mane and taped it into her scrapbook. Tuck had teased her about keeping a "baby book" for a horse. She'd just frowned at Tuck and kicked his shins. He had yelled "Boss Mare" and dodged away from Meg.

On the day of the match race, Tuck delivered a mountain of newspapers to Meg.

"Look at the front pages of each and every one of 'em," Tuck said, thumbing through the pile. "Ruffian. All Ruffian."

Meg smiled, "She's the face of the women's movement, that's for sure. Check this out, 'Girl Power: Ruffian.'"

"Yeah, Ruffian's sure to win. I'd bet all my money on her." Tuck rustled through the newspapers. "Foolish Pleasure came from a po-dunk Florida town—smack dab in the middle of nowhere. Nothing but live oaks, alligators, and skeeters." He chuckled. "He don't stand a chance."

"He won the Kentucky Derby," she reminded him.

"Yeah, but then he placed second in the Preakness and the Belmont. He couldn't clinch the Triple Crown."

"What's his pedigree?"

"Got some Bold Ruler blood in him," Tuck answered.

"Like our girl."

"Um-huh. Except Ruffian has Native Dancer in her, too. Double the speed," Tuck acted like a proud papa.

Meg studied the black and white news photos of Foolish Pleasure. His knees weren't the best. He also seemed heavy-bodied. Yet he had won all seven of his starts as a two-year-old.

"Hey, get this, Meg," he added, "he sold for $20,000 as a yearling."

"Cost don't matter much. It's talent and drive." Meg mumbled, "He might be tough to beat."

"Hey, what's going on with you? Don't you have faith in our girl?"

"Sure I do…but something don't feel right." Meg chewed on her bottom lip. "I don't know. Maybe just race day jitters."

Tuck, trying to perk her up, went on, "I heard the winner gets a big fat paycheck. About $225,000. Is that true?"

"I don't know. Frank doesn't talk money around me. Just with the Janneys."

"Not bad take-home pay if she wins."

Mike came up to them, "No time to be fussing over the papers. Meg, you got a horse to get ready. There's about 50,000 people in the grandstands. All cheering for Ruffian."

Tuck added, "And probably 20 million people watching her

175

on TV."

Keep your mind on the race ahead, Meg told herself to settle her nerves. She thought about all Frank had said in the days leading up to the race. *A foolish match race. A marketing gimmick. Not right to pit two youngsters together. One of 'em is gonna burn out,* he said. Meg tried to shake her uneasiness but she'd come to trust Frank's instincts.

All Meg remembered about the rest of that day is this: Rushing into the paddock, handing Frank the saddle. Frank cinching it around Ruffian. He checks the buckles, tests the reins, her bit. Ruffian stands stock still, like a fine statue, only her ears twitch in anticipation. Meg strokes Ruffian's neck, soothing herself more than the horse. She feels butterflies in her stomach. Not because she's afraid Ruffian might lose. Losing is bound to happen to all of them, sooner or later. Meg frets over other things, like injury. Real trouble.

Before Meg realizes it, Jacinto hoists himself into the saddle. Off he and Ruffian go to the track. As usual, Meg positions herself near the rail at the far turn to watch.

The crowd sounds like a tidal wave as Ruffian loads into the starting gate. Foolish Pleasure is in his gate.

The gate springs. Ruffian stumbles. She leaps forward, regains momentum, and charges ahead. A gladiator.

Ruffian is on the rail. Big red Foolish Pleasure on the outside. Stride for stride. Neck to neck, keeping pace, galloping, galloping, galloping, pushing ahead a nose, a head. More. And more. *And more.* Jacinto lets her run. And run. And run.

A shift. Ruffian leans into Foolish Pleasure. There's a large crack like the sound of a falling tree. Ruffian pulls back. Foolish Pleasure pulls ahead. Away, away, away. Ruffian's furious. She has never lost. She must lead. She must win. She fights to regain the lead.

She's galloping.

She's galloping.

Pounding the dirt.

Running, chasing

Him. She must win.

Jacinto pulls

and pulls, pulls

the reins.

To stop. Stop.

Meg prays and weeps, *Hold up, girl*

Hold up, slow

Please, girl.

Stop, girl

Jesus. Stop.

Whoa, girl

Easy

Easy

Girl.

Ruffian, at last, stops on the track. Blood pours from her leg. She dances, dances in terrible circles. Her eyes white-rimmed. Screams spill from her. Screams spill from Meg.

CHAPTER 27

Emergency

Vet Clinic

Belmont

3:30 a.m.

The incandescent light shone on the worn-down faces of Meg, Frank, Tuck, and Mike. Frank sat, head in his hands, immobile. Mike leaned against the clinic's filing cabinet, wiping his eyes on his coat sleeve. Meg crouched in the corner, knees tucked into her chin, face buried in her arms. They'd been at the clinic all night after Ruffian broke down. Meg felt as if she were trapped in a gauzy fog, unable to push her way through to find any source of light, of hope.

Camera flashes punctuated the dark of night. Hungry reporters wanted to be the first to seize the breaking news about the world's fastest filly. Mike chased them away from the clinic, promising them news about Ruffian just as soon as he had it. The clinic needed calm and quiet so the vet team could repair Ruffian. Mr. and Mrs. Janney were there too, for a time, until Mrs. Janney broke down, wailing in grief and pounding her fists on Mr. Janney's chest. After they'd gone, Frank acted as the go-between, calling the Janneys before the vets administered another best effort procedure to try to save Ruffian.

All Meg could remember, what she couldn't shake, was Ruffian's banshee screams as the sounds of her hooves pummeled the walls of the surgical room. If this is what hell sounded like, they were there. Ruffian thrashing in pain, her screams ricocheting across the vet clinic. Meg wanted to escape or, most of all, go back in time before Ruffian even loaded into the starting gate. She wanted to stop the match race from ever happening. *Who really cared who the fastest horse was anyway? It didn't matter. Nothing really mattered. Nothing at all. Just Ruffian.*

Doc and three other track vets worked all night, trying to repair her destroyed leg. Trying, trying so desperately to save her. Meg heard the men shouting at one another. *Easy. Steady. Another painkiller. Hold her. Watch it. She's kicking. Get back. Outta the way. She'll kill us all.* Through it all, Ruffian shrieking. They'd told Meg not to watch. They told her to go on home. They told her. But she couldn't. When the team had Ruffian sedated enough for surgery, the clinic was silent. As quiet as a morgue.

Meg stood up on her tiptoes to peer into the surgical room. A green, ghastly glow shrouded the doctors and they bent over the long table. Meg saw a large equine form covered with a gray cloth. Ruffian. Finally still. Heavily medicated for surgery. The doctors worked swiftly, trying to repair the bone, the hoof, the carnage. Doc deftly cast the leg. *Will it hold? Could she stand on it? Would it hold her weight?* Those were the questions. Not many horses survived an injury of this sort. Ever. Most horses would have been shot on sight, to end their suffering. Not Ruffian. Meg knew that the Janneys and Frank's team loved this filly. She loved this filly. Ruffian had been her reason for breathing these past two years.

It was all Ruffian. It always was. Without a doubt. And none of them would have it any other way.

"Anethesia is wearing off," Doc yelled to the team. "We need to move her to the recovery stall. Now. Get over here." Doc waved his arm to the men, signaling them to each help lift the filly to carry her to the recovery room. "It's padded in there. In case she wakes up thrashing." Doc didn't get two more words out of his mouth. Ruffian's head jerked upward. Her eyes opened. Meg gasped. Ruffian's eyes were glassy, white rimmed, and wild. Her left leg shot forward. "Get back!" Doc yelled as Ruffian's legs punctuated the air between them.

Another voice shot out, "Shock! She's in shock!"

"Hold her down!"

"Get the hell back! She's gonna kill us!"

The shrieking. The death call.

Meg cried out, "Help her! Please!" She covered her mouth and her face with her hands. The thundering intensity of Ruffian's fight echoed through them.

"She's smashed the cast," a voice shouted.

"She's smashed her leg to hell!" another wailed.

More banshee shrieks rang from Ruffian.

Meg crumpled to the floor.

• • • • •

"Call the Janneys," Doc yelled out to Frank, "We gotta put–"

Frank knew what needed to be done. Outside the recovery room, he clutched the telephone in his hand.

"Stuart, it's bad. She ain't gonna make it. No way. She went through surgery but came out thrashing, smashed it all to bits."

Mr. Janney didn't let Frank finish the details. "Do what must be done. Put the poor girl out of her misery. Don't let her suffer anymore."

Gone. She was gone.

• • • • •

Belmont Race Track

9 p.m.

Headlights illuminated the race track gravesite. Frank, Mike, Jacinto, Doc, Tuck, and Meg circled the grave. Ruffian, shrouded in a lily-white cloth, was lowered into the earth. Her head pointed toward the finish line. Clear silence enveloped the small gathering. Frank handed Mike two cherry-red Locust Hill blankets. His voice cracked, "Here, Mike, go put these on her."

Mike climbed down into the grave and lovingly laid the barn's blankets over Ruffian's still body, smoothing the blankets over their girl, taking as much care with her in death as they did in life. Someone, Meg didn't know who, laid a single red rose onto Ruffian's body.

"Anyone care to say a few words," Mike asked as he climbed out of the grave, wiping back the tears from his eyes.

"She was the finest damn horse I ever got to ride," Jacinto whispered.

Meg, fighting her sobs, said, "I love you, girl. I love you."

181

Mike wrapped his arms around Meg, squeezing her, trying to comfort her.

Frank, never a man of many words, put his hat back on his head and added, "The best horse I could have ever hoped for." He wiped his face with his handkerchief. "Come on, crew. It is done."

The headlights flickered. Fireflies danced in the darkness. A tractor engine rumbled, ready to move the earth across Ruffian's grave. Meg let out another sob. Doc came to her side, "Come on, sweetheart. Let's go home." Doc took Meg by the arm, leading her from the grave. Her world was gone. Ruffian was gone.

CHAPTER 28

And So It Goes

Back at their own barn, routines had to be kept. Everyone reported back to work. There were other horses to tend to, ones that were alive and well, untouched by the tragedy. Ones who needed to be fed and watered and exercised. "So it goes," Frank told his team before they began the morning duties. "So it goes." Meg saw Mike's chin tremble. He was choking back tears. Meg, and everyone else for that matter, hadn't slept for days, and they stood numb in the early dawn light. Home. At last. But without their girl.

They moved through the feeding schedule like sleepwalkers. Plodding, silent, solemn. By lunch, Frank, Mike, Tuck, and Meg sat in Frank's office, still too heartbroken to eat. Doc, coming in from his medical rounds, joined them. His face sagged with exhaustion. To Meg, her uncle looked old for the first time.

"How are you doing, kid?" Doc asked her.

Meg blinked, trying to focus on Doc's question.

"Meg?"

Frank said gently, "Kid, you ok? You've been through a lot."

The horsemen circled Meg. Doc put his arm around her shoulders. She quivered and then she coughed. Then she wept.

Mike, the first to speak, tried to console Meg, "She was one of a kind. And there'll never be another one like her."

"We were blessed to know her," Frank said.

They searched but couldn't seem to find any more words.

It was Doc's words though that stuck to Meg's heart. "We are graced with these creatures. For a short time. It is our responsibility to care for them—with dignity and compassion. No matter what."

Meg looked up at her uncle. She wiped her eyes. She saw clearly. "We did that. Always. Didn't we?"

The men nodded and wrapped their arms around their girl.

● ● ● ● ●

The days that followed were not easier. A heavy sadness hung in the barn, wrapping them in silence. The normal barn banter between the grooms had ceased. Each barn hand moved as if in a trance, mechanically going about the chores, feeding, watering, shoveling. They couldn't shake the loss of their mighty girl. Meg had reported to work each day, just as everyone else had. No matter how hard it hurt their hearts, they had horses to care for. This evening, Meg was measuring out supplements in the feed room. She had to give out the vitamins intended to keep the racers strong and healthy.

Doc came into the room and leaned against a grain bin. He crossed his arms over his chest. "How you doing, kiddo?"

Lifting her eyes from the measuring container, Meg saw a raw sadness in her uncle's eyes. Even for a seasoned vet like Doc who helped animals into the world, and eased their journey out of the world, it was impossible to not mourn Ruffian's death.

Clearing his throat, he said, "You ever heard of *Anam Cara?*" Doc, leaning closer to Meg, went on, "It is an old Irish phrase. Means 'soul friend.' Someone who understands you and sees you without any sort of mask. Where you find home."

Meg whispered, "Ruffian."

"Yes, ma'am. You were two of a kind. You just knew something about her, and she you. A sacred friendship, if I ever saw one."

"*Anam Cara,*" Meg repeated, rolling the ancient words around in her mouth. "What happens when your soul friend dies?" She asked it from the deepest thread of her soul.

Doc shrugged. "Wish I had an exact answer for you…" Doc stopped, looking Meg squarely in her eyes, "Honor her spirit by tending to other horses just as you did her. Don't be afraid of loving others. Give your heart, kid. Give it to the world." Doc tugged at the ends of Meg's ponytail. "Got it?"

"Got it."

"You know what else?" Not waiting for Meg to answer, Doc gave Meg a bear hug. "You can have human soul friends too, kiddo. You can always turn to me and Aunt Louise if you ever need folks to lean on."

Meg let herself sink into his hug. She felt like a little bitty girl, a girl lost and alone but clinging to this person, this person who shared her sorrow and wanted to be her support through it all.

Doc, lifting Meg's chin up in the crook of his finger, said, "Better get back to work."

Meg nodded, thankful that her uncle understood. She returned to measuring the supplements. She couldn't take her mind from Doc's words: *Anam Cara*. Soul friend. Her Ruffian. She doubted if she would ever have another friend like that horse.

CHAPTER 29

Friends

Lexington, Kentucky

December 1975

"Meg, get the door!" Mrs. Murphy shouted from the laundry room.

Ding dong ding dong ding.

Meg flew down the stairs, "Coming, for Pete's Sake!"

Who in their right mind would be hammering their doorbell at 7am on a Saturday morning?

Flustered, Meg flung open the front door.

Tuck.

He had a cat-that-swallowed-the-canary grin on his face. Meg was instantly suspicious. Tuck liked to pick and play. What game did he have in mind today?

"Morning, Meg. Got a minute?" Tuck stepped inside the Murphy's doorway, closing the door behind him. She took a step back.

"Nice pajamas," he smirked, pointing at her Wonder Woman night gown and matching slippers.

She furrowed her eyebrows, "What do you want at this hour?"

"I heard it's your birthday."

"It's not my birthday."

"Yes, it is. And I have a delivery for you. If you would put on a bathrobe and step outside."

Meg snatched her mother's coat from the back of the armchair, closing it around herself. Tuck grabbed her hand and dragged her out the door. There was a rusted-out stock trailer sitting in front of her mailbox. Tuck led Meg a smidge closer, whispering, "Happy birthday, cuz. Happy birthday."

As Meg got closer to the trailer, she saw two familiar brown eyes, eyes the color of coffee, watching her from the slats in the trailer. Long, brown, velvet ears flicked in her direction. She felt a tug at her heart. A feeling she hadn't felt in a long time. Then, there it was, a long, high whinny of welcome.

Tuck unlatched the stock trailer door and swung it open. "Whatcha waiting for? Climb in."

Meg was shaking as she stepped inside.

"Do you like what you see?"

Standing before Meg was a shaggy chestnut horse.

Buckwheat. Her Buckwheat.

How could it be?

She thought he was long gone, working as a trail horse back in Montana. Buckwheat neighed to Meg and pulled at the rope.

"Does this mean you're happy or should I return this gift?" Tuck joked as he saw tears springing in Meg's eyes.

Wiping her nose on the sleeve of the coat, Meg croaked out, "HOW?!?"

Tuck, rather sheepishly, said, "I remembered your story about him. Doc and Louise did, too. We tracked him down. Wasn't too hard. A few phone calls. The ranch was willing to let him go for a song—after we told 'em how much you missed him and what had happened with you and Ruffian. They said, 'No gal should be without a horse she loves.'"

Touched and confused by such a grand gesture, Meg asked, "Why?"

"Since… you know…you didn't seem right, you know after…" Tuck shuffled uncomfortably on his feet. "Doc said he'd pay for the board on this horse—if you'll keep helping him on his rounds. A will-work-for-food kinda deal."

Meg pounced on Tuck, wrapping him in a surprise embrace, "Thank you." She squeezed him hard.

"Easy," he laughed, "I ain't a grapefruit. Go love on your horse. He missed you."

She untied Buckwheat from the trailer and backed him down the ramp. Once unloaded, Buckwheat whinnied another greeting to his girl. He raised his head in the air, calling to her. Meg threw her arms around his thick neck and just held the horse tight. Buckwheat craned his neck around her as if hugging her in return. Meg walked alongside Buckwheat, scratching him from behind his ears, down his neck, moving her fingers down his side. The horse practically purred under her hands. He gave a great shake of his body. Utter, complete delight.

"Hey there, kids!" Doc hollered out to them as he pulled up in his truck. Aunt Louise barely waited for the truck to stop before she hopped out. She had a brilliant red halter and lead rope in her hands.

"Happy early birthday, Meggie! You surprised?"

She rushed into her aunt's arms. "Thank you."

"Happy early birthday to you, happy early birthday to you," Mr. and Mrs. Murphy sang as they carried a chocolate cake toward Meg. Sophie nestled on Mom's hip.

• • • • •

Spring 1976

Dewdrops sparkled on the grass. Song birds called from the trees. Squirrels chittered and chased each other in the branches that hung over the horse trail. Buckwheat ambled through the sandy trail that wound up and around the farm, edging past the pastures filled with broodmares. On his back sat Meg. She rode bareback. A nice, easy pace. Sometimes leaning forward to pat Buckwheat on his neck. Other times, to lean way back and stretch her back along his spine, feeling the warm sunshine on her face. Buckwheat swished his tail from side to side as they walked. Meg was glad he was content with his new home. There was nothing she loved better than these Sunday mornings. Sometimes Tuck would join them with one of the barn's exercise horses. When Tuck did, he would always bring apples for the horses for afterwards and chocolate for the humans. She didn't mind having Tuck around. What she loved best though was when it was just her and Buckwheat. Her fella. He made everything all right.

What was the phrase Doc had told her of? *Anam Cara.* That was it: *Anam Cara.*

Photo Credit: Adam Coglianese, Track Photographer, of the New York Racing Association.

Epilogue

Churchill Downs

May 29, 2018

Meg pushed her mother's wheelchair into the grandstand area. Sophie, balancing a tray of coffee and donuts, followed behind them. Mrs. Murphy shifted her body in the wheelchair. She leaned forward, pointing to the marquee. "Those sportscasters have got it all ready to live broadcast, don't they?"

Meg muttered a "um-hum" as she navigated the ramp down to the track's rail, dodging deep, muddy puddles left from the early morning rainstorm. Sophie helped Meg make the turn at the end of the ramp, to better position their mother at the track's rail.

"You see okay, Mom?" Meg asked.

Mom folded her hands in her lap. "Front and center. Best seats in town." She sounded delighted.

Sophie passed out the morning's breakfast. Aunt Louise hustled down the steps, singing, "There you are, gorgeous gals! I thought you ran off after I dropped you at the front gate!" Sophie offered Aunt Louise a powdered donut and a coffee.

Meg checked her watch. 7:20am. They'd made the road trip from South Carolina to watch Justify train. Justify had already won the Kentucky Derby and the Preakness. He stood a good chance of winning the Belmont Stakes, securing the Triple Crown. The four women crowded the rail, nibbling on donuts and strong coffee. "There he is," Meg whispered, pointing to a massive chestnut colt prancing their way.

"My, oh my, he is huge," Sophie said through a mouthful of donut.

The exercise jockey slowed Justify in front of the women. Justify turned his full attention to them. His ears pricked forward. His eyes were steady and determined. Yet it was as if he looked right through them. Meg's breath caught in the back of her throat. *Fierce.* She remembered that look.

"What is it?" Sophie asked her.

"He's going to win the Triple Crown," Meg said without a doubt in her mind.

"You can't know that," Sophie pointed out.

"Oh yes I can. I've only seen that look on one other horse before—and that was on Ruffian."

Shivers ran down Meg's spine as she remembered her years with the big, beautiful filly. Ruffian, her girl, her girl with the fighting heart. Ruffian's focused gaze before a race. Her confidence, her fire. Meg remembered how awful it was to say goodbye to her.

"God, was she a horse," Aunt Louise whispered and slid her arm around Meg's shoulder, pulling her close.

Meg took a sip of her coffee, hoping it would warm her. "That she was." Her fingers felt the locket around her neck, the locket that held a wisp of Ruffian's mane and a wisp of

Buckwheat's mane.

"Here's to Ruffian and to all the fine horses everywhere," Sophie said, raising her coffee cup in tribute. "And here's to fine vets like our Meg and Uncle Doc who look after them."

The women raised their warm coffee cups into the crisp spring air as a parade of brilliant horses breezed by.

RUFFIAN
1972–1975

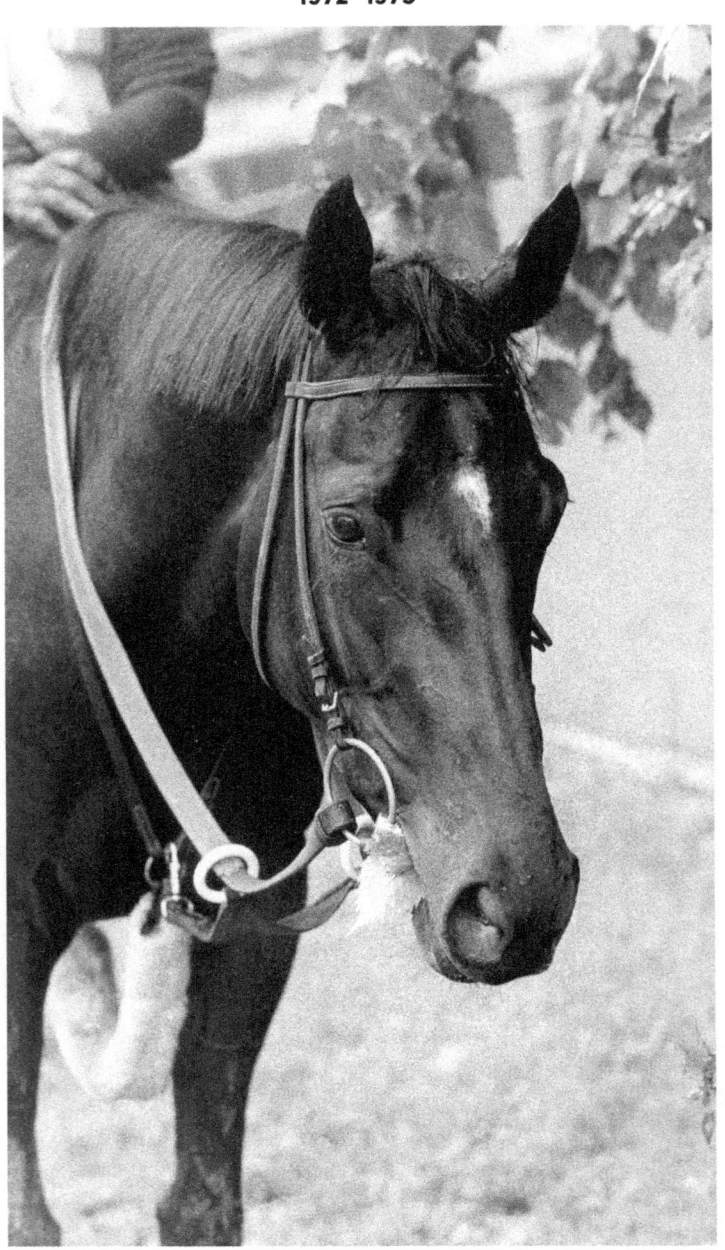

Sunday, July 6, 1975, Belmont Park, New York:

The New York Racing Association promoted a match
race to see who was the fastest horse in the United States. The
Association wanted the Kentucky Derby winner Foolish Pleasure,
a colt, to run against the Triple Tiara winner Ruffian. This race
would determine who was Horse of the Year, who would go into
racing's Hall of Fame.

Over 20 million people watched the race on American
television. Fifty thousand people crowded the stands at Belmont.
Fans cheered wildly for the spectacular filly as they led her to the
paddock. Jockey Jacinto Vasquez had won the Kentucky Derby on
Foolish Pleasure but he chose to ride Ruffian for this match race.
For many American women, Ruffian symbolized the grace, power,
and strength of the women's movement. If Ruffian won, American
women won. Ruffian seemed to sense how important she was.
She strode around the paddock area, sleek, powerful, looking
at the spectators squarely in their eyes. She was determined,
confident, ready to win. During the race, Ruffian got injured. She
had to be euthanized. America had to say goodbye to the fastest
filly in the world. Ruffian is buried, nose pointed toward the finish
line, ready to win it all, at Belmont Park.

Finest Filly Facts

Ruffian won ten consecutive races, earning over $313,000 in her short career.

1974 Eclipse Champion 2-Year-Old Filly

1975 Eclipse Champion 3-Year-Old Filly

1976 Hall of Fame

Since her tragic death in 1975, the horse racing industry has made tremendous strides in equine medicine. Today, recovery pools are often used as horses come out of anesthesia to prevent injuries from thrashing. Yet racing injuries still occur.

Anatomy of a Horse

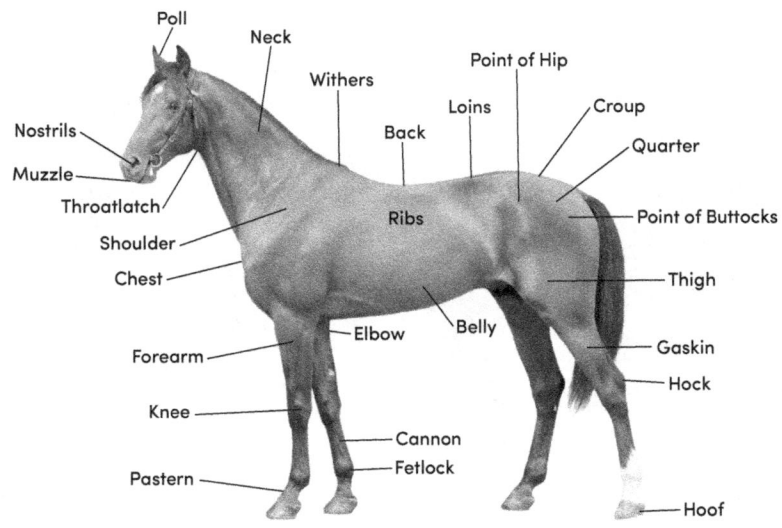

Racing Glossary

Filly: a young female horse that is under five years old

Furlong: an eighth of a mile, or 220 yards

Groom: a person who takes care of horses

Jockey: a person who rides horses in races

Maiden Race: a horse's first professional race

Mare: an adult female horse

Paddock: an area near a race track where horses are kept

Pastern: part of the horse's foot just above the hoof to the fetlock

Stakes Race: a race where prize money is given out to the winner

Starting Boxes: large chutes where racehorses are loaded right before the start of a race

Racing Tack

Timeline

APRIL 17, 1972

Foaled

Claiborne Farms
Paris, KY

NOVEMBER 1972

Yearling Training

Raceland, KY
with John Sosby

NOVEMBER 12, 1973

Secretariat retires to
Claiborne to Stud

*Out of
Rehab*

AUGUST 23, 1974

*Saratoga
Spinaway Stakes*

Against
Laughing Bridge
1:08.3 Bracciale

JULY 27, 1974

Sorority Stakes

Aganist Hot N Nasty
1:09 Vasquez

APRIL 14, 1975

*Aqueduct
Allowance Race*

1:09 Vasquez

APRIL 30, 1975

*Aqueduct
Comely Stakes*

1:21 Vasquez

MAY 10, 1975

*Aqueduct
Acorn Stakes*

1:34.2 1-mile
Vasquez

NOVEMBER 16, 1973

Ruffian to Frank Whiteley
in South Carolina

*Two-Year
Training*

1974

Bigger than
Secretariat

○ ○ ○

JULY 10, 1974

*Aqueduct
Astoria Stakes*

Against
Laughing Bridge
1:02.9 Bracciale

JUNE 12, 1974

*Belmont
Fashion Stakes*

Against Copernica
1:03 Vasquez

MAY 22, 1974

*Belmont
Maiden Race*

1:03 Vasquez

○ ○ ○

JULY 6, 1975

*Belmont
Match Race*

Against Colt
Foolish Pleasure

*Died
July 7, 1975*

MAY 31, 1975

*Aqueduct
Mother Goose Stakes*

1:47.4 1 1/8 mile
Vasquez

JUNE 21, 1975

*Belmont, Coaching Club
American Oaks*

2:27.4 1 1/2 mile
Vasquez

○ ○ ○

NOTES

As I researched Ruffian for this book I found many newspaper and magazine articles about the horse and the people who worked with her. I attempted to honor their memories as accurately as possible. Even though this is historical fiction, I would like to specifically give credit to the following quoted materials found in the novel.

Chapter 6

"Girls can be ruffians too." As found in Jane Schwartz's *Ruffian: Burning From the Start*, p. 110.

Chapter 9

For more on Ruffian's saddle training, see Milton C. Toby's *Ruffian*, pp. 17-23.

Chapter 13

"Have you ever seen anything like her?" Yates gasped... as found in a *Sports Illustrated* article, "The Lady Is A Champ," by Tex Maule, a woman was quoted as saying, "You ever seen anything like her? She's not real." *Sports Illustrated*, May 19, 1975, p. 66.

"The horse wanted one thing: To run." In a *Lexington Herald* newspaper article from July 8, 1975, Bill Lyon wrote: "She knew only one thing—run." Np.

An account of Frank Whiteley and Yates Kennedy's work with Ruffian is found in Jane Schwartz's *Ruffian: Burning From the Start*, pp. 76-80 and pp. 88-89.

Chapter 16

For an actual account of Frank Whiteley and Jacinto Vasquez's meeting , see Jane Schwartz's *Ruffian*, pgs. 65-68.

Chapter 19

"Ruffian sets her own pace and gets there on her own." Jacinto Vasquez said this. As found in "Ruffian (horse)," *Wikipedia,* updated 11 September 2017, accessed 7 December 2017, https://en.wikipedia.org/wiki/Ruffian_(horse).

Chapter 20

"I didn't do nothing…" Jacinto answered. As found in *Sports Illustrated,* July 1975, Vasquez actually said, "When she heard those horses, she took off. I didn't have to do anything." Np.

Chapter 21

"She moves like a Cadillac when you ask for more gas." For the record, Jacinto Vasquez said, "She's like a gold-plated Cadillac….Like a Caddy when you ask for more gas, no?" As found in Milton C. Toby's *Ruffian,* p. 48.

"Each race she taps into another gear we didn't know she had." In a real interview, Jacinto Vasquez said, "She had gears not too many horses have…" As found in Scott Davis, "Along for the Ride," *The Blood-Horse,* June 24, 2000, p. 3845.

"…I never really let her run, you know." Vince Bracciale told this to Jimmy Dailey, as found in Jane Schwartz's *Ruffian: Burning From the Start,* p. 157.

See Jane Schwartz's account of the race against *Hot N Nasty in Ruffian: Burning From The Start,* pp. 131-136.

Chapter 27

"Don't let her suffer anymore." Mr. Janney told this to Doc Harthill before Ruffian was euthanized. Found in Steve Haskin, "Frank and Forthright," in *The Blood-Horse*, June 24, 2000, p. 3839.

"Here, Mike, go put these on her." Frank Whiteley said this to Mike Bell at the burial: "Here, you put them on her." As found in Bill Nack, "Hoofprints of the Century," *Thoroughbred Times*, July 8, 2000, p.66.

Bibliography

Anderson, Dave. "Ruffian Just Keeps Rolling On And On." *The Courier-Journal & Times Sunday Edition*, 1 June 1975, Section C 10.

Biles, Deirdre B. "Grasping At Straws." *The Blood-Horse*, 24 June 2000, pp. 3847-3849.

Boyd, Eva Jolene. "Matchless Ruffian." *Spur*, July/August 1991, pp. 74-79.

Cady, Steve. "Ruffian Is Buried Near the Finish Line in Belmont Park Infield." *New York Times*, 8 July 1975, www.nytimes.com/1975/07/08/archives/ruffian-is-buried-near-the-finish-line-in-belmont-park-infield.html. Accessed 7 December 2017.

---. "Ruffian's Demise Calls Attention To Plight of Lesser Race Horses." *Lexington Herald*, 15 July 1975, p. 9.

Cox, Teddy. "Find Ruffian's Measurements Even Overshadow Secretariat's." *Daily Racing Form*, 9 September 1974, p. unknown.

---. "Ruffian vs. Sarsar. Never, Says Yates." *Daily Racing Form*, 1 July 1975, p. 41.

Davis, Scott. "Along for the Ride." *The Blood-Horse*, 24 June 2000, pp. 3845-3846.

Durso, Joseph. "'Why' on Ruffian? Maybe the Change in Dirt's Texture. *The Courier-Journal*, 8 July 1975, Section B8.

Goldstein, Herb. "Ruffian In Her Own Class on 'Record.'" *Daily Racing Form*, 16 June 1975, np.

"Hall of Fame Trainer Did Things His Own Way: Frank Whiteley Jr., 1915-2008." *Lexington Herald-Leader*, 3 May 2008, np.

Harthill, Alex. "Ruffian Twice 'Revived From Dead' by Various Means in Vain Attempt to Save Filly Champion." *Daily Racing Form*, 9 July 1975, np.

Haskin, Steve. "Frank and Forthright." *The Blood-Horse*, 24 June 2000, pp. 3835-3840.

Hillenbrand, Laura. "Ruffian: Only the Legend Lives." *Thoroughbred Times*, 1 July 1995, pp. 18-19.

Hollingsworth, Kent. "One Great Filly: When They Talk About Great Racehorses, Fillies Are Often Overlooked, But How Does One Ignore Ruffian?" *Thoroughbred Times*, 12 February 1993, pp. 22-23.

"Jacinto Vasquez." National Museum of Racing and Hall of Fame. Updated 2016. www.racingmuseum.org/hall-of-fame/jacinto-vasquez. Accessed 7 December 2017.

Johnson, William Oscar. "Could She Have Been Saved?" *Sports Illustrated*, 21 July 1975, pp. 20-24.

Kindred, Dave. "The Filly-Colt Match Ended in Tragedy As…The Lady Ran Out of Luck." *The Courier-Journal*, 7 July 1975, page 1 and back page.

"King Filly." *Time*. 2 June 1975, Sports Section, np.

Layos, Allie. "Unmatched Legacy: The Tragic Story of Ruffian the Racehorse." *Wide Open Pets*, www.wideopenpets.com/the-tragic-story-of-ruffian-the-racehorse/. Accessed 7 December 2017.

Lifshin, Lyn. "On the 30th Anniversary of Ruffian's Last Race." *Equus*, https://equusmagazine.com/horse-world/ruffian_070805. Accessed 1 January 2018.

Lynch, Pat. "Vasquez Memories of Superfilly Ruffian." *Thoroughbred & Harness Racing Action*, 6-12 October 1988, p. 23.

Lyon, Bill. "Ruffian's Spirit Cost Her Life." *Lexington Herald*, 8 July 1975, np.

Mann, Jack. "It Ended With One Fatal Step." *Sports Illustrated*, 14 July 1975, pp. 16-17.

---. "They'll Burn From The Start." *Sports Illustrated*, July 1975, pp. 24-29.

Maule, Tex. "The Lady is a Champ." *Sports Illustrated*, 19 May 1975, p. 66.

Milbert, Neil. "Death of a Beauty." *Lexington Herald-Leader*,

9 July 1999, Section C9.

Nack. William. "Pluperfect." *The Thoroughbred Record*, 12 October 1974, pp. 1118C and 1122.

---. *Ruffian: A Racetrack Romance*. ESPN Books, 2007.

---. "25 Years." *The Thoroughbred Record*, 12 July 1975. Reprinted in *The Thoroughbred Times*, 8 July 2000, p. 66.

Nagler, Barney. "Ruffian's Fate A Terrible Loss To Horse Racing." *Daily Racing Form*, 9 July 1975, np.

Phelps, Frank T. "A Brief, Brilliant Career." *Sun Herald*, 7 July 1975, np.

Reed, Billy. "'Chances Were Nil.'" *Louisville Courier Journal*, 23 July 1975, np.

"Remembering... Ruffian." *Horse Racing Nation*, www. horseracingnation.com/news/Remembering_Ruffian_123#. Accessed 7 December 2017.

"Ruffian." *National Museum of Racing and Hall of Fame*. Updated 2016. www.racingmuseum.org/hall-of-fame/ruffian. Accessed 7 December 2017.

"Ruffian (horse)." *Wikipedia*. Updated 11 September 2017. https://en.wikipedia.org/wiki/Ruffian_(horse). Accessed 7 December 2017.

"Ruffian (1972-1975)." *Claiborne Farm*. http://clabornefarm. com/halloffame/ruffian/. Accessed 7 December 2017.

"Ruffian's 'Friends' Bemoan Loss." *The Lexington Leader*, 7 July 1975, p. 1.

"Ruffian's Owners Invited to Bury Her at Horse Park." *The Lexington Leader*, 7 July 1975, p. 1.

Schmitz, David. "Complete Review." *The Blood-Horse*, 24 June 2000, pp. 3852-3853.

Schwartz, Jane. "A Runaway For Ruffian." *Sports Illustrated*, 9 May 1988, np.

---. *Ruffian: Burning From The Start*. Random House, 1991.

Shulman, Lenny. "Her Glory Marches On: Ruffian Remembered 25 Years Later." *The Blood-Horse*, 24 June 2000, pp. 3831-3833.

---. "For Whom The Bell Tolled." *The Blood-Horse*, 24 June 2000, pp. 3841-3843.

Smith, Gene. "Ruffian." *American Heritage*, September 1993, www.americanheritage.com/content/ruffian. Accessed 1 January 2018.

Toby, Milton C. *Ruffian*. Eclipse Press, 2001.

Tower, Whitney. "She's Just Like One of the Boys." *Sports Illustrated*, 2 September 1974, pp. 49-50.

Wilkinson, John. "Ruffian's Last Dance," *Horse Network*, https://horsenetwork.com/2015/07/ruffians-last-dance/. Accessed 7 December 2017.

Note on the Author

Precious McKenzie lives in Montana with her family. Ever since she was a small child, Precious was horse-crazy. Thankfully, her parents encouraged her love of horses. They told her that when she grew up and got a job, she could have a horse of her very own. So she did. Precious is the author of over thirty nonfiction books for kids. She keeps busy with her American Paint horse. She loves to research, write, and teach, and is dedicated to sharing the amazing world of animals with kid- readers.

9 781735 364117